BURN THE BRIDGE

by ARQUIE

To the women expected to put others first.

Chapter 1

My little sister's fingers twisted my pant leg as she ground her forehead into my thigh. "Don't go, Brin," she sobbed. "Please don't leave."

My throat tightened, and I cleared it so my voice wouldn't waver. "I'll come back for you. I promise."

My brother stood behind her with his eyes on the floor. He was only a few years younger than me, and at that age he dashed away his tears and set his jaw instead of giving me a hug goodbye.

I promise…

"Which one do you think he'll like?"

I inhaled with a start. As the distant memories faded, I studied the dresses in front of me. "Blue would be more appealing."

Princess Rhofe's dainty nose crinkled. "Red suits my complexion."

I pursed my lips behind the safety of my headdress. If Rhofe saw my displeasure, her confidence would crumble. Feigning boredom, I turned her around to pin the remainder of her light brown braids. Both dresses were too over-the-top for my liking, but the other handmaidens had convinced her to woo the Prince of Sadary with extravagance.

For me, it didn't matter much if Rhofe succeeded in catching Drevan's eye, only in entertaining him for the night. My bag was packed and stowed safely in the cellar. Some called it treason—I called it good riddance.

My sister's wobbling lip flashed in my mind, and I clenched my jaw. Going forward would lead me back.

Alfy, Rhofe's dove familiar, looked up from preening his new feathers as a pin dropped to the floor. He rested on a gilded perch in the corner, studying us with rapt interest. After tonight, it'd be a relief to never have to see another glint of the dreadful metal.

Hillcrest's greatest asset was the thick veins of gold threaded through the vast mountains, but a thousand years ago, we dug too deep. Poisonous gas erupted from the mines, spreading across the kingdom in a deadly fog. A once-thriving kingdom fell to ruin almost overnight. Some of our ancestors with familiars survived by climbing to the tops of the mountains where the gas was thinner, and some were fortunate enough to ascend peaks high enough to escape the fog altogether.

It'd been almost seven hundred years since Hillcrest's royals had sent the lower class back into the mines. The mist burned our skin, eating away at our nerves and mobility until we no longer had the strength to feed ourselves. We became a little more immune with each generation, but non-lethal didn't make it pleasant.

Rhofe tossed the red dress to the side and started pulling the blue one on. Even though she struggled, I didn't help her. The other handmaidens would have, but Rhofe kept me close because she knew my assistance was near nonexistent. It was her way of reclaiming a sliver of independence.

Heg, my honey badger familiar, padded to the door and sniffed at the torchlight spilled underneath. My fingers curled to brush the hilts of the daggers hidden in my sleeves.

With a deep sigh, Heg shook her head. *They're having roasted quail at the feast,* she said in my mind.

A smile tugged at my lips, and my hands relaxed. *Always one for quail, aren't you?*

What? She snorted with proud indignance. *Tasty little fowl.*

Rhofe cleared her throat. "Brin, would you mind…?"

Nodding, I laced the back of her dress. I didn't mention how I needed to tighten what she'd already done. Corsets were hard enough.

Heg brushed past my ankles and made for the sill of the open window. The flickering flames danced with the last rays of sunset, but nothing could beat the fresh autumn breeze swirling around the room. Curtains almost as thin as the princess's dress billowed along the stone floor.

With a shy smile, Rhofe lifted her arms and twirled with gentle grace. Dusty blue fabric embroidered with gold flowers flowed down her body, and a deep neckline drew attention to her breasts. She'd get cold with the loose sheer sleeves, but such was the price she'd pay tonight.

At least the handmaidens' attire was more useful. My plain black clothes were sized up to allow free movement but cinched at my wrists and ankles to limit an opponent's advantage. Two flat daggers were strapped to the insides of my forearms, two more at my ankles, and one gaudy gold knife on my belt. The gold was fake, but it drew enough attention to my hip instead of my hands to give me a slight advantage. A leather pouch was looped next to it, holding a flat oval stone with black runes in the witch language etched along the sides.

The article setting us apart, though, were our headdresses. A simple black cowl hung over my head, and a slip of additional fabric crossed over my face to cover all but my amber eyes. The fabric fell loose past my arched nose before tucking into my tunic. What spells Hillcrest could purchase to fight against the gas were stitched with more runes in dark thread at the hem of the material. Not that they helped much, but none of the other castle folk were afforded such a luxury.

Handmaidens had to go wherever the princess went, even if she was captured and taken into the mist. Attacks didn't happen often, but we were trained in many ways in service to the crown to earn our keep.

"Brin?" Rhofe played with a golden flower by her thigh.

I narrowed my eyes with a hardened gaze, and whatever she meant to ask died on her lips. Dropping the fabric, Rhofe straightened her back, and a swell of pride unfolded in my chest.

When I'd passed the standards to be accepted as a handmaiden, I'd started out like all the rest and pandered to her comfort. After a few months, I'd realized I needed to stand out if I didn't want to be sent back down the mountain. My way of achieving that was giving her what she craved: a sense of power.

Rhofe's body was a bargaining chip, and her fate had been sealed before she was born, so her mind was all she had left. Undoing eighteen years of conditioning was slow going, but my efforts weren't in vain.

"My parents wish for me to enter after Prince Drevan has been seated. A willing bride rushing into her lover's arms," Rhofe said with cool indifference.

I crossed my arms, a hint of a smile playing at my lips. "And?"

Her mind whirled behind a calculated mask. "I want you to sneak me into the Grand Terrace before he arrives." Adjusting her hair with an air of confidence, Rhofe said, "I represent Hillcrest. If he sees me as weak, he'll take advantage. I want him to come to me. Kiss my ring. Bow to me. I am a ruler in my own right, and he will see me as such."

"Sneaking about in your own palace is a weakness," I replied. "Retrieve the other handmaidens from the kitchens and walk through the halls with your head held high."

Rhofe turned with a wary slowness. Alfy flew to her shoulder and rubbed his head along her jaw. Stroking a finger over his sore wing, she said, "Mother will hurt Alfy again."

Frustration swallowed my usual reservation. Everything needed to go according to plan, regardless of which persona Rhofe decided to present.

If I didn't find a way to help my siblings, they'd be condemned to a life in the mist, but the castle wasn't the saving grace my parents had thought it was. Alganise, the kingdom to the west and a short journey from Hillcrest, seemed like a good opportunity to secure a safe place to bring my family to.

All I had to do was play my part for a few more hours, slip away in the dead of night, and cross the bridge without being caught. The castle guards would be focused on the Sadarians and escorting drunken nobles to their chambers, so if Rhofe's defiance took more eyes off me, it was a win.

I bent to retrieve one of the shorter knives from my ankle. Scanning for the best place to hide it, my eyes locked onto the heap of braids cascading down her back.

"Hold still," I said. The sharp blade nipped a few strands, but I wedged it in until it was concealed.

"What are you doing?"

I turned Rhofe's shoulders so her eyes peered into mine. "If that wretched cat goes after Alfy again, you kill it. Your mother will live, and she won't be able to retaliate if Drevan goes through with the marriage."

Rhofe's lip wobbled, and my breath hitched.

She's not your sister, Heg murmured. *You don't owe her anything.*

I'm not doing this for her. We need an ally out there, and she'll be in Sadary soon enough. My words were hidden behind practical strategy, but deep down, I cared about Rhofe. It was difficult for me to grapple, though, because she'd been born to never touch the mist, while my family was drowning in it. Why did I care about Rhofe's troubles, when she didn't acknowledge the suffering of her people?

Heg's ears flicked. *I hope you know what you're doing.*

So do I.

Tapping Rhofe's temple, I said, "Clear mind, remember. All those what ifs and maybes are bees in your head. Make a decision and box everything else up until you've traveled the path you need to. Process when you're in a space you can."

Rhofe crushed me to her chest and squeezed. I let her stay for a few seconds before stepping away.

Rhofe swiped at her tears and licked her lips. "I suppose it's now or never."

I tilted my head, not confirming or denying. She needed to take the risk on her own, or her gall would wither from worry.

Looking for a bit of courage, Rhofe drifted over to the bed and slipped a slim book from under her pillow.

I sighed. "You have to let go of legends, Rhofe. Your fated mate will not suddenly appear, sweep you away, and save you from your duty."

"I know that," Rhofe snapped. "But I refuse to lose the one bit of hope I have in this prison."

I held back the wave of anger boiling in my heart. These walls weren't only bars for her. Eight days. It'd taken me eight days in her service to understand the gravity of how many basic necessities other kingdoms had, while our people scraped together scraps. Out there, people worked for currency, not rations, which they could trade for anything they wanted in the other kingdoms.

If the mines in Hillcrest met quotas, the workers were rewarded with better equipment to boost production in the next cycle. Food, water, and supply rations were doled out occasionally, but were never increased. In the castle, favorable standing with the royals or usefulness to the kingdom determined the generosity of material goods.

Rhofe placed her saving grace in fairy tales. I placed mine in plans.

Heg licked her lips. *They're almost ready for eatings.*

"If you want this to work, we need to go now," I told Rhofe.

The princess flipped through the pages until she landed on her favorite: a gilded image of a brilliant sun illuminating an embracing couple. The woman had a streak of red in her blonde curls, while the man had a strand of light in his burnt amber hair. A small hedgehog was depicted by the woman's foot, and a snowy white owl glided over the man's head. Their familiars seemed as happy as they were. Fated mates, chosen by destiny.

I resisted the urge to snatch the book and smack her over the head with it. The only true stories in Hillcrest were the ones they told children to get them to behave.

Rhofe trailed gentle fingers over the page before she stashed the book, straightened her dress, and nodded. "Let's do this."

"Why are you waiting for me?" I waved at the door. "You want to be queen? Act like it."

Hurt flashed in Rhofe's eyes.

With a low growl, Heg hopped down from the sill and padded towards the princess. One swipe of my familiar's paw at her ankles sent her stumbling for the door with Alfy flapping his wings to keep balance.

"Follow me," she said. Her voice sounded too forced, but it'd have to do for now.

Chapter 2

The wide cobblestone hallways were lined with blazing torches and open archways. Fresh air was taken for granted here, and a familiar sense of guilt washed over me for every inhale that didn't feel like glass tearing into my lungs.

I'd been born in the village at the base of the mountain, near where it dropped off into the gorge. Forced to work alongside my father in the mines, we dug into the belly of the mountain and hauled out anything of value we could find. At fifteen, my parents scraped everything they had to bribe my way into the castle and pave a better future for my brother and sister. It'd taken two years to earn a place among the handmaidens, and three since.

Sometimes on quiet nights, the breeze carried pained cries up from the village. Their misery kept me staring at the rafters into the early morning, and my vigil helped soothe my guilt at leaving my siblings behind. Although, the gnawing ache never really went away.

I kept a step behind Rhofe and to her right as she led us deeper into the castle. Heg's breathing became labored as she sucked in more of the delicious smells. The edges of the white stripe along her back rippled over her ribs with every inhale. Even with the distraction, she remained alert. Her nubby ears flicked to attention with every small sound, and her short tail lowered with calm caution.

The guards didn't pay us any mind, but I kept track of them regardless, as there were more than usual. Two were posted at each archway, and patrols of four marched through the halls in cycles. Everyone knew everyone in the castle. It was unsettling to see more faces I didn't know than did. Some had been taken from the bridge, some from other castles, and the rest were probably Sifters.

Eventually, a swell of heat indicated our arrival to the kitchens. Heg perked up at the sight of crispy skin and glistening fat droplets roasting on spits.

An odd assortment of staff milled about the wooden counters, roaring fires, and casks of fine wines. Off-duty guards clad in gold armor, handmaidens in all black, and the castle tradesmen bustled about. Even the children of the court helped cut vegetables and stir soups.

Space at the top of the mountain was limited, creating a social ecosystem where everyone in the castles needed a purpose. Some became masters of their trade, while others became indispensable at multiple skills for fear of being sent to the mines to be more useful.

"To me," Rhofe demanded in a clear, commanding voice. Perhaps she could pull this off after all.

The handmaidens gracefully passed their duties to the others before stepping in line behind Rhofe. Their familiars slipped from the corners and followed on their heels. It wasn't uncommon for there to be more than one of the same familiar, but each of the six handmaidens had a different type to protect the princess as best we could. Among the handmaidens were a phoenix, a fox, a black bear, an anaconda, a wolf, and my honey badger.

None of us had long-term romantic partners due to our involvement with visiting nobles and other guests, but a few spent their time in good company of castle folk. The spymaster used what we learned to better influence the rest of the realms. Despite Hillcrest's lack of an army and strength of numbers, the queen's vast network of ambassadors and spies spun tales of a strong kingdom with riches beyond compare.

Before the mist, Hillcrest had actually been wealthy. We'd earned well-established relations, especially with the covens due to trading crystals for spells. The more powerful witches were bonded to familiars, and a few Hillcrest nobles paid to be bonded to a familiar as well. At first it was meant to be a status symbol, but as time went on, and the practice became more popular, our people began finding their fated mates.

To have a familiar was to have a torn heart. Once in a lifetime, a person would meet someone whose frayed heart would fit with theirs. Strands of hair would exchange, and the natural magic of their familiars would flourish under the song of a harmonic pairing. It was said fate never made a mistake, so who wouldn't be drawn in by the hope of a life full of love and happiness?

Children came easy to fated mates, and to everyone's surprise, a piece of the baby's heart manifested outside of their body to become their own bonded familiar. Eventually, most of Hillcrest was convinced a familiar was a sound investment, despite the steep cost. Word spread to the other kingdoms, but they had little to offer the covens. Hillcrest seized advantage of their dismay and dove deeper into the mines to sell them crystals to trade to the witches. All was well—until the mist came.

Our demise was widely seen as a bad omen. Only warrior kingdoms like Sadary and a few undeterred romantics pursued familiars afterward. The witches mostly kept to their own. Not shunned, but not welcomed, either.

All descendants of fated mates were born with familiars. Through the years, our ability to meet our fated mates was limited by the lack of travel between mountaintops and the rate of perish in the mines. I assumed death on the battlefield created the same issue for Sadary. Eventually, fated mates faded into legend.

Rhofe's confidence seemed bolstered by having her handmaidens around her, or maybe it was because she still clung to the hope Prince Drevan would be her fated mate. She swept out of the kitchen and made for the Grand Terrace.

I narrowed my eyes. The long way would take us in a loop around and only reach the doors at the last second.

With a glance, I confirmed only a pair of guards posted ahead would see my boldness. There might be more around the corner.

"Rhofe, take the northern hall," I said under my breath.

Alic, the handmaiden on my left, shot a glance towards me while her phoenix circled above. With a three-foot wingspan and feathers the color of red-hot iron, the bird was hard to miss.

The princess's stride halted. "That's too much time in the open."

"It takes us through the guest wing," I argued back, my voice merely a whisper. "The servants will talk. Let them."

"My lady may take the route she wishes," Alic joined in.

I glared, and she matched my fire.

Rhofe's indecision warred on her face.

"The safest option would be to return to your chambers and wait to be summoned," Taalyn murmured. Her brown spotted anaconda lounging across her shoulders flicked his tongue in agreement. Although she was the youngest handmaiden, she'd earned her place among us with how much magic her familiar lent her. Having the snake shrink to accommodate her small frame was a casual spell most of us wouldn't have been able to sustain for long.

Heg gravitated closer to my calf while frustration threatened to rip away my cool mask. Part of my lack of compassion towards Rhofe's weakness was calculated, and part was simply because I didn't care to coddle her. I had my own life I needed to protect.

Rhofe had to play her part for one goddamn night. It seemed a fair trade for the years I'd been in her service. I needed Prince Drevan to accept her hand, so Rhofe needed to pick a personality.

The princess glanced between the three of us and chewed her bottom lip. Hardening my stare, I lifted my hand and tapped my temple.

"Alic, Taalyn," Rhofe said, wiping her sweaty palms on her dress. "Follow Brin's lead."

Fuck, I swore as she led us along the northern route.

What's she tryna do? Heg huffed. *Start a pissing war between her handmaidens? It won't help her cause tonight.*

Or ours, I grumbled. Rhofe should have shouldered the command on her own instead of ruffling the others with giving me false authority.

Heg looked up, annoyance plain in her black eyes. Taalyn's anaconda flicked his tongue, and Heg bared her teeth. The other handmaidens' expressions were hidden behind their headscarves, but their familiars said quite enough with raised fur and sidelong looks.

Rhofe ignored our silent bickering and strode with her head held high. The guards straightened when she approached, and servants who usually paid her no mind lingered around corners to catch a glimpse of the princess.

I stopped paying attention to Alic trying to keep one step ahead of me when we entered the guest wing. Unfamiliar black leather armor adorned these guards instead of the bright gold ours wore. It almost looked like snakeskin, although their familiars were all the same ordinary types of animals we had.

My fingers unconsciously curled towards my hidden daggers, but I forced them to stay loose. Heg's claws tapped a little louder on the stone.

None of the Sadary nobles were visible, but a girl carrying a pile of blankets hurried into a chamber with a lit hearth. Hopefully in combination with the others we'd seen, rumors would spread. If Prince Drevan was smart, he'd have his spymaster send out his servants to spark up conversations with ours.

Rhofe flicked her wrist at the guards ahead. Rich, dark wood banded with gold-plated steel stretched high above us. The guards pushed the heavy doors open.

The Grand Terrace was constructed as an open platform jutting out from the mountainside. A servants' staircase was hidden along the edge to give guests an illusion of privacy with the closed doors. A dozen columns of white marble were set in two rows along the edges of the terrace and reached for the open sky. Shining statues of familiars of past rulers rested on the flat tops. Most would think they were made of solid gold, but Hillcrest was desperate enough to keep their decorations superficial.

Wisps of clouds floated in the sky, blotting out all but the full moon and the brightest stars. The castle and little squares of orange clung to the mountain. Corridors with open archways leading to tall turrets and inner rooms were carved from stone found deep within the mines. Beyond the careful work of builders long past, rough, raw rock covered the mountainside.

A gust of cool air fanned the braziers between the columns, feeding the flaming shadows creeping up the marble. I should have been able to smell the smoke.

Heg raised her nose, and I nudged her with my foot. *You better be using my scent for more than quail.*

Heg's head bobbled. *There's a trace…*

My middle finger grazed the hilt of a dagger. *What is it? Foreign.*

Does it smell Sadarian? Like the guest wing? I could have sworn Heg rolled her eyes.

All at once, smoke crammed down my throat and expanded in my chest until it hurt. It consumed me from the inside out, burning my nostrils and searing my lungs. I swallowed a cough and scowled at my familiar.

Heg's low chuckle echoed in my mind as the smoke faded.

That's not funny.

Heg preened. *That's up to interpretation.*

While I'd been preoccupied, Rhofe stepped forward between an aisle made from a pair of long tables. A third table was set lengthwise before four thrones. Dinnerware carved from rubies lay on the well-oiled wood, and gold-plated chalices marked each placement.

The largest throne, chiseled from obsidian and inlaid with an arc of sapphires, sat in the middle while the other three were more like plain gold seats. Queen Crysul had arranged two gold seats on the left for her and the king, and one by itself on the right of the obsidian throne. Isolating Rhofe was the queen's attempt to diminish her confidence and make her look like a meek, willing bride.

My hands tightened into fists. I hated feeling powerless.

Cellar. Bridge. Freedom.

Rhofe's fingers trailed over her chair before she hardened her face and sat in Prince Drevan's seat.

My lips slid into a small smirk. I liked this side of her. With the princess settled, two handmaidens joined the guards, two hid behind the columns, and I stayed behind the thrones with Taalyn.

Alic's phoenix circled above, and Heg wove around the columns. Alfy perched on the black throne, a speck of innocence in a room that'd soon fill with anything but. Only the crackle of burning logs broke the thick silence.

Rhofe pinned her gaze on the door, awaiting her future with a brave face.

Heg's comment nagged at me. If there was an opportune time to ensure Hillcrest's decline, tonight was it. Living in the castle wasn't always easy. There were occasional mutinies from miners who climbed the mountains. The trolls in the south were never friendly, and the goblins in the east had once kidnapped the queen when she was a child for ransom. Not to mention the flood of thieves from the stories of grandeur we spun to conceal the truth.

The future of Sadary and Hillcrest, as well as both our allies, rested on a marriage of alliance and a treaty of prosperity. Hillcrest had relations with Oppanuk, known for its blacksmiths and crafters, while Sadary traded with Vadril, bountiful with acres of fields and large herds. Due to proximity and longstanding bad blood, Oppanuk and Sadary had been at war for some time. It wasn't the only war Sadary waged, but it had taken the heaviest toll.

If all went well tonight, Hillcrest would have an open line to Vadril, and the violence between the other two kingdoms would end peacefully. Of course, a healthy payment of gold would also fund Sadary's remaining campaigns.

There were those who didn't see that as a beneficial prospect, and I didn't know enough about the outside world to know who they were, or how far they'd go to tip the scales. Our orders had simply been to take extra caution.

Unable to stand still, I joined Heg, making a pass around the room. My steps slowed as we approached the railing. Far below, blips of torchlight lit the only feasible pass out of Hillcrest—Dridgeton Bridge.

The bridge created safe passage to a secondary, smaller mountain. A deep gorge plunging through the valley was filled with mist too thick even the strongest of my people wouldn't be able to survive if we tried to travel across the bottom. The bridge had been built high, but the underbelly still kissed the lazy swirls of green. Natural rock formations jutted out along the edge of sides of the far mountain, keeping the worst of the gas contained.

As I watched, two torchlights went out at the top of the nearest tower. Mostly everything else was blurry with the distance and the dark, but a few moments later they blinked back to life.

They don't usually replace them two at a time, Heg said.

Even if they're shorthanded? Some of the guards might have been pulled up here.

Doubt it. Heg's nose twitched, and she swung her head to catch the wind.

Any luck with the scent? I asked.

It's a tickle I can't seem to sneeze, she muttered. Drifting away with her eyes closed and nose in the air, Heg wound through the columns to make another lap.

Movement at the edge of my vision had me whipping out the gold knife. I whirled around in a crouch, but it was only a line of servants appearing from the kitchen door at the base of the steps.

The judgement in Taalyn's eyes as I made my way back to the thrones caused heat to rise to my cheeks. Feeling a bit sheepish, I sheathed my knife and clasped my hands behind me. The nerves would be my undoing if I couldn't control them.

Only a few more hours, I told myself.

The servants piled the tables high with roasted vegetables, ripe fruit, and warm meats. I found myself grateful Heg had taken my ability to smell as the lavish sight bothered me enough.

Familiars and humans were linked in thought and spirit, which let magic flow between us freely. Most of the time we could harness it into spells with practice. Communication was the first spell mastered with a familiar. Enhancements, like sharing senses, were also fairly simple, but I wasn't as good with the other spells. Endurance came with experience, like running or fighting.

I've lost the trail. The food has blotted it all out, Heg complained.

It's okay, I assured her. *Stick close, and we'll be alright.*

The white along the top of Heg's head bobbed as she sniffed the railing. *Maybe we should have waited for the queen. I don't like this.*

Can't go back now.

Across the room, Alic tossed a log into a brazier a little more forcefully than necessary. She held my gaze, conveying her disagreement with the plan. She had family at the bottom of the mountain, too, and if the treaty didn't go through, rations would be cut until the royals figured out what to do. Or not at all, but we both refused to entertain that possibility.

Footsteps and clinks of armor echoed in the halls. Rhofe dropped her hand from where she'd absentmindedly been stroking Alfy and took a steadying breath.

"Queen Crysul with her familiar, Jekell!" a steward announced as the doors opened. "And King Renn with his familiar, Medge!"

Rhofe straightened her back as her parents and their guards entered. Both royals dripped in brilliant yellow. The queen wore a shimmering gown with sleeves one could almost believe were dipped in gold, while the king opted for a white doublet embroidered with wings of rich ochre thread.

Jekell, a lion with a black-tipped mane, prowled at Crysul's side. Medge flew past them with a rush of wind, gliding up the columns and landing on the back of a stag statue. The bald eagle perched above, leveling us with a threatening eye.

Rhofe's knuckles went white under the weight of all four gazes. Alfy hopped back onto her shoulder and tucked his head under her jaw.

"It seems our daughter wishes to spoil this union before it's even begun." Crysul ran her fingers over Jekell's head, and his tail twitched.

Renn kept his features disinterested. "Prince Drevan will not arrive for another half hour. Taalyn, take the princess back to her chambers. This evening will resume as planned."

Taalyn reached for her, but Rhofe stood and threw off her hand. Turning to her parents, she said, "This is a feast in my honor. My marriage. My future. You will sit or have no place at all."

Taalyn's anaconda struck at Alfy. The dove bolted, taking to the open air to escape. I stayed put, even when Medge dove. Even when her talons snatched up Alfy, and Rhofe flinched.

I could only work from the shadows. Whisper in the right ears and plot in the darkness. Anything outright, and they'd throw me down the mountain, or worse—put me in the mines again.

Rhofe reached for her braids. I stepped forward and grabbed her wrist before she could make more of a mess of things. The hurt of betrayal splashed across the princess's face, and my nostrils flared with annoyance. Couldn't she see I was trying to save her cards? Revealing the dagger now would be fruitless.

"My, my." The voice was low but stole our attention with a whisper. "What a quaint little family."

Chapter 3

Prince Drevan stood in the center of the doorway. He looked to be in his early thirties, but maybe war had aged him more than he was. A crown of woven black leather rested on his dark curls, giving off a slight but unmistakable air of power. He glanced around until his silver gaze landed on my hand around Rhofe's wrist.

I released her. *Shit.* So much for the first impression being strength. Now we had to go with demure.

The prince didn't look like most royals, and a sense of apprehension grew in my gut. Other royals feasted and pleasured and struggled to move their bloated bodies. Their kingdoms were ripe with art, music, and peace.

Prince Drevan's body was clad in black armor like his guards. The swell of muscles he'd earned fit well on his tall frame. Nicks and scars peppered the skin along his hands, face, neck, and no doubt other parts currently concealed. A chain whip made from sharpened metal scales looped over his belt, but I couldn't find his familiar, and unease crept up my neck.

Sadary was a kingdom of war. A future with him was not a happy one, but one I needed my ward to accept, nonetheless.

"Meek," I whispered.

Anger burned in Rhofe's eyes. "Prince Drevan, how very interesting you find yourself here, at this hour, in this room…when you clearly have not been summoned."

The faintest hint of a smile drifted over Drevan's face. "Dear princess, don't believe your illusion of power. I could shit on your plate, and have you lap it up if I pleased."

I stepped in front of her, my brows furrowed with a scathing glare, and raised my dagger.

Heg straightened her legs to make her appear taller and trotted out from the columns. *Who the fuck does he think he is talking to her like that?*

Drevan raked an unimpressed gaze over my tense form and the girl taking refuge behind me. His head tilted with intrigue.

"Release the dove," he commanded.

Medge shrieked in defiance and landed on another stature with Alfy still clutched in her grip.

Renn narrowed his eyes. "You do not command me or mine, princeling."

Drevan grabbed his whip, turned once, and snapped it into the air. Shadows raced over the metal, and an arrow soared towards Medge. No, not an arrow. A serpent. Drevan lowered his arm, whip still in hand and poised at the ready.

I pressed Rhofe back until the throne bumped into her knees. She clung to my arm, her nails leaving little crescents through my tunic.

Drevan's familiar struck Medge in the neck and wrapped its body around hers. She screeched and tried to peck it off, but the snake wrapped itself out of reach. The zing of an unsheathed sword rang out.

Renn leveled the weapon at the prince, a vein throbbing in his temple. Was the snake's venom lethal?

Since a familiar was manifested out of only a piece of our heart, a human could live without a familiar, but a familiar couldn't live without a human. Most pain was shared, but physical wounds to one did not hinder the other. With the magic pouring from Drevan's whip, though, I wasn't sure what we were up against.

A cold dose of fear washed over me.

Drevan brought his whip down and knocked the sword from Renn's hand. Metal clattered on stone.

"I won't ask again," Drevan said in a calm, hard tone.

Medge screeched again but loosened her talons. Alfy tumbled a few feet before righting himself. Rhofe jumped to catch him and clutched him to her breast.

"The trade terms will be amended," Renn spat. "We will not—"

Brin! Behind! Heg scrambled to reach my side.

I ducked on instinct, missing the club whooshing past my head as the ground trembled under my feet.

"Taalyn!" I yelled.

Taalyn shoved Rhofe towards her parents while I assessed the threat.

Spittle splattered the marble as an ugly, nearly naked troll roared. Hundreds of steel teeth poked out from the bulging end of his club, and a belt of bones held up his fur loincloth.

Another troll swung over the terrace railing and bounded up behind him. Both were almost as tall as the columns. A company of a few dozen humans and their familiars joined their accomplices before we could do much of anything.

They had plain clothes, plate armor, and well-made weapons. Either their sigils had been stripped, or they were hired.

How'd they get the sneak on us? I growled.

Probably some nasty little silence spell, Heg hissed.

I clenched my jaw and tried not to think of anything beyond the now. Regardless of my escape, my duty was to protect Rhofe and make sure this proposal went through.

I focused on my heartbeat. The quick rhythm and the pulse in my ears. I blocked out the rush of guards and the shouted orders until I could hear Heg's heart pounding with mine. I steadied my breathing until a light tingle tickled my eyes and ears.

When the troll raised his club again, everything sharpened. The wrinkles on his bulky fingers. The flare of his nostrils. The bits of old blood left on the steel spikes.

He swept his club low, intending to wipe out my feet, but I danced out of reach. A brazier tipped, and embers scattered over the floor. Angry now, the troll pounded his club into the column on his left. Marble crumbled, and a golden creature crashed to the ground in a cloud of straw and clay.

I didn't hear it. I couldn't hear anything. While Heg took my ability to smell and hear, I took her vision.

Whipping around, my gaze flicked about the room. Medge tore at the second troll's head. An empty eye socket and half his face were a bloody mess. Renn and Crysul were surrounded by their guards, but most of them were dead, and four handmaidens circled Rhofe. One of the trolls had knocked a column across the doors, trapping us with the mercenaries.

Although we'd reacted as well as we could have, panic was plain in our ranks. Trolls attacked the southern castles on occasion, but they never ventured this far north. With their size and proximity to the mist, they'd built immunity right alongside us. The soldiers outnumbered Drevan's guards and the small escort the royals had.

Someone who knew both our weaknesses planned this.

Sweat trickled down my back, and I furrowed my brow. I refused to die fighting for a kingdom like Hillcrest. If I fell tonight, it'd be for family.

The troll in front of me lifted his right heel, and his fingers clenched around the club's shaft.

Taking my chance, I raced forward. He didn't have time to bring his weapon down or adjust his balance by the time I'd slipped between his legs and jumped.

My dagger sank into his calf to hold me up. Not wasting a second, I flicked out a dagger from my sleeve and sliced the back of his knee. My blade was sharp, but his muscles were thick. It took me three swipes to do the damage I intended with one.

Trying to shake me off, the troll stamped his foot and danced in a circle. I gritted my teeth while Heg tore at his other ankle to distract him.

A flash of steel was my only warning to move. Abandoning my dagger, I dropped to the floor, and the arrow intended for me buried itself in the troll's calf. Turning his vengeful glare on me, the troll swung his club in a sweeping arc.

I scrambled behind the remnants of the pillar, which promptly became demolished rubble. Diving forward, I barely missed the club smashing down again. Stone and hot coals skittered across the floor, and embers seared my hands and feet. I kicked them aside and struggled to regain my balance.

Two mercenaries—one with a bow, one with a sword—a hyena, and a raven boxed me between them and the troll. Heg tackled the hyena with a fierce growl and latched onto its throat.

I risked a glance behind. The handmaidens and I had our disagreements, but at the end of the day, we shared the same struggle. We all wanted a better life for ourselves and those we loved. I cared about their safety almost as much as Rhofe's.

Taalyn's anaconda, now ten times its natural size, struck the troll behind me and began wrapping its body around his chest. With his weapon neutralized, the troll tried to rip away the snake with his free hand.

I focused back on my own fight. Taalyn and her familiar were a formidable force; they could handle the troll for now. I hissed as an arrow sliced my cheek and clattered to the floor. Wetness glued my headdress to my skin.

The sting faded with the rush of the fight as I kicked coals into the soldiers' faces. The raven dove, beak stretched open in a silent screech. Rather than raise a blade, I followed my momentum, planted my leg, and kicked my other foot up.

The impact threw the bird off course. Before it could right itself, Alic's phoenix flew past and latched onto it. The raven hit the ground missing a head.

The soldier holding the bow grimaced and nocked an arrow for the phoenix. Throwing my dagger, the blade speared his throat, and the man joined his familiar on the bloody floor.

When the second soldier whirled on me with a raised sword, I charged with nothing but curled fists and a war cry. He swung a diagonal cut. My second sleeve dagger found his heart, and the writhing hyena grew still in Heg's jaws.

The Grand Terrace was a bloody mess with bits of stone and bodies strewn everywhere. My throat tightened at the destruction, but I couldn't linger.

Process when you're safe. I told myself.

The trolls were occupied with Medge and Taalyn's anaconda, and tremors vibrated through the floor as a grizzly and half a dozen men surrounded Prince Drevan. His whip carved a red circle around him.

Good. Let the mighty warrior earn his keep.

I searched for Rhofe, grasping onto the hope we could somehow salvage this disaster. The princess's mouth opened in a scream that didn't reach my ears. Crysul's lion pounced on Rhofe, and while Alfy escaped into the air again, the princess reached for her braids.

A moment later, droplets of blood sprayed across Rhofe's face. My feet moved without thinking, and dinnerware shattered as I scrambled across the tables. I couldn't stay on the sidelines of this any longer.

Jekell's fangs flashed in the firelight. A crimson slash marred the fur above his eye, but he seemed otherwise unharmed. His paw smacked the knife from Rhofe's hand, and it skittered across the floor into the fray.

The other handmaidens engaged themselves elsewhere, as if the only threat they cared about came from the soldiers.

I rammed into the lion headfirst. Claws sank into my ribs, and I gasped at the raking pain. They sank deeper, ripping across bone. We rolled, and up became down until my head smacked stone.

Then the claws disappeared, along with Jekell's weight. Coughing, I pushed onto my back and wheezed. Jekell tucked his head and clawed at the shadowed rope around his throat.

Thankful for the distraction, I flipped to my belly and crawled to Rhofe with a hand pressed against my side. My vision blurred at the edges, and specks of white decorated the rest.

Four handmaidens had guarded Rhofe. Three remained. Tillip's fox was dead, and the rest were holding off the dozen or so mercenaries trying to get to the princess. With the attackers focused on Drevan as well, their intentions to destroy the alliance were all but plain.

The troll with half a face backhanded Medge with a triumphant bellow and charged towards us. The bald eagle crumpled to the floor.

HEG! I cried.

I blocked out the wave of burning agony in my ribs and pushed to my feet.

He was ten steps away.

Panic rattled my chest.

Seven.

Terror consumed Rhofe's features.

Three.

The troll raised his club.

One.

Wrapping my arm around the princess and tucking her tight to my body, I dropped the stone from my belt to the floor. A shield of magic from the runes circled me as Heg gave back my senses and my body froze into place.

My honey badger grew…and grew, and grew, until she was half the troll's height. A cold, biting prickle nibbled at my skin from the Surging spell as Heg barreled into the troll with a menacing yowl. Her claws scraped bloody grooves into his torso, and she tore off his ear with a snarl. He shoved her away and slammed his club into her stomach.

Pain blossomed in my gut, but I couldn't move, couldn't do anything but watch as Heg used her body to protect us. I screamed at my muscles in silent agony, but it did nothing to make them obey. Arrows flew in our direction, and not even the threat of death could force me to dodge before they shattered against the shield.

I wasn't as good as Taalyn with Surging yet. She could move freely with an enlarged familiar while I couldn't. Our resident witch had imbued a spell into the stone to protect my body temporarily while Heg Surged. Since Rhofe was next to me, the small shield protected her as well, but Alfy was out of my field of vision, and I couldn't move my eyes to find him.

Blood trailed down Heg's underbelly, which only fueled her ferocity. She clamped onto the troll's bicep and tore at his arm until his flesh was reduced to ribbons.

Bellowing with rage, he beat the back of her head with a closed fist. Red streaked through white along her back, and pain pounded through my pulse.

A few paces away, Alic battled three soldiers with her phoenix. One slipped past her guard and slammed his sword into my shield. The second blow cut through the spell, and his blade sliced into my thigh.

A scream died in my frozen throat.

Rhofe struggled out of my grip and shoved the mercenary. Before he could harm the princess, a blast of flames from Alic's phoenix engulfed his body. Heg turned from the troll and brought her paw down on the burning man, reducing him to a puddle of blood and bones.

With my familiar distracted, the troll swatted Alic's phoenix to the ground.

"No!" Alic gasped, falling to one knee.

Heg lunged for the troll's throat, and with a snap of her jaws, she clamped down until the troll went slack. The castle rattled as my familiar brought him down.

Not wanting to leave me undefended, Heg released the Surge and shrank to her original size before she ran to help Alic.

A rush of tingles pricked my skin as the spell wore off. Stumbling through it, I snatched a stray sword and Rhofe's arm while I backed away.

Taalyn and her anaconda were still fighting the remaining troll, but his writhing form was on its way to being dead. Rhofe's parents and their familiars fought off the last few attackers on our side of the room. Drevan kept the grizzly and its human at bay but had killed the other soldiers past the tables. Alic and Heg were protecting the phoenix's unmoving form from a soldier and his wolf.

The other handmaidens had been eliminated.

As much as I disliked it, I shoved my knife in Rhofe's hand and pulled her toward her parents. We'd be safest with them. My leg burned, and hot pokers stabbed into my side.

Jekell threw a soldier into the nearest column and stalked towards us. He licked his maw, putting his fangs on display.

Rhofe froze. "No," she whispered. "Don't make me go with him."

Heg yelped, and searing white pain sliced into my spine as the wolf bit into Heg's neck. I ripped out of Rhofe's hold and shoved her towards her mother's familiar.

"Stay with them!" I ordered.

"Brin!" Alic and Rhofe cried out.

My head whipped between them as terror raced through my veins.

Jekell latched onto Rhofe's dress and dragged her down. Red splattered across my boots as maroon slashed through Alic's neck, and she crumpled to the ground. The soldier tugged his ax from the handmaiden's body and brought it down for Heg's head.

A desperate scream tore out of me, and I threw the sword at him. It didn't do any damage, but the flat edge was enough to knock his aim. Still, he managed to engrave a nasty gash behind Heg's ear.

Looking up, the soldier took in the bodies of his fallen comrades and a handmaiden coming straight for him. His wolf threw Heg down and raced to the far end of the terrace. Straight towards the servants' stairs.

Oh, no, you don't.

As the man sprinted after his familiar, I reached for the last knife I had. My vision sharpened. Sound faded, and the knife left my hand.

Chapter 4

In a stroke of unfortunate luck, the soldier had learned from the sword. My dagger sailed over the railing while he disappeared down the steps.

"Fuck," I breathed.

Heg didn't waste another moment. Despite her wounds, she raced after them. I clenched my teeth and forced myself to keep on her tail. We chased the soldier down until I slammed the door open to the kitchens.

The guards and tradespeople so lively an hour ago were slumped over the counters with glassy eyes. Vegetables were strewn across the dirty floor, and the spits had been smashed to bits. My breath hitched as dread took root.

I tried to move through the carnage, but a discarded pot tipped me off balance, and my palm slapped down on the nearest surface to steady myself.

A small finger brushed mine. No more than ten, a young girl looked up with frightened eyes and blonde hair slicked to the sides of her face. She'd used the counter to prop herself up with one hand, and the other cradled a sword slice through her stomach. Blood soaked the oversized apron she'd never grow into.

"It's going to be okay," I whispered, drawing her into me. "It's all going to be alright."

Smoothing her hair out of her face, I gave her the only mercy I could. I wrapped her in a hug and snapped her neck. Bees buzzed in my head, telling me it was my fault as I lay the girl down and closed her eyes.

If I'd been able to kill the soldier, the girl might still be alive. I shouldn't have pushed Rhofe tonight. If we'd been in her chambers, we wouldn't have been trapped on the terrace, and then we'd have had more guards come to our aid. What was I going to do now? Would I be able to protect my sister, or would she die because of me, too?

Pushing to my feet, I trapped the bees in a box, shoved it to the recesses of my mind, and reassessed the situation. Those worries wouldn't help me now. Heg was already at the door, nose in the air. I took a breath to steady myself and hurried to catch up, even as pain spiked through my leg with every step.

Anything? I asked.

Both hallways were empty. No guards stood at their posts, but no bodies littered the area, either.

Heg paced at the threshold. *Nothing,* she whined. *No. No. NO. I can't smell anything but quail!*

I knelt and rested a hand on her back to still her. *It's okay.* I pressed my forehead to hers. *It'll be okay.*

I didn't know if I was trying to convince myself or her. She licked my cheek. *We should go, slip out before things settle. The wolf man is gone.*

My eyes drifted to the trapdoor to the cellar. Heg was right. I eyed her neck and stomach. *You sure you can make it?*

I will if I have to. She nuzzled my hand onto the doorframe, and I leaned against it to climb to my feet.

Before I'd made it a few steps, a young guard rushed down the terrace steps and burst into the kitchen. An osprey flew through the door and landed on his outstretched hand. I tried to keep the guilt from my eyes and angle my body away from the cellar, but I wasn't sure if he caught it.

"Harol." I nodded in greeting. He'd always been kind to me. "One got away. Go back up. We need to protect the princess."

Harol frowned. "You're hurt."

I tried to wave him off, but my leg buckled under the sway. His osprey flew back through the door as Harol rushed to my side.

"I got you," he said as he threw my arm over his shoulder. Slowly, taking care to go easy with my wounds, we picked our way back up the stairs.

I should have been more upset with losing our chance to escape, but the truth was, I didn't think we would've made it. My eyes were heavy with exhaustion, and it took everything Heg had to crawl up the steps alongside me. We needed to rest and reevaluate.

The Grand Terrace was destroyed. Pieces of shattered marble, gold, and remnants of dinnerware littered the ground. Half of it was cast in shadows from the strewn braziers, and red smears painted the stone between pools of blood.

But the bodies. I swallowed the bile rising in my throat. The fortunate souls had been taken by a blade. Most had been mauled by claws, teeth, and talons.

I paused over Taalyn's empty stare. Her anaconda had managed to swallow half of a troll before my fellow handmaiden had fallen from an arrow.

I forced myself to look at the others. The black clothing hid most of the blood, but not the cuts. Mental replays of the battle consumed my mind. If I'd dealt with the troll quicker. If I'd—

A bright orange feather floated atop the puddle of red from Alic's body. I fell to my knees. Two trolls. Three score of men—trained men, at that, with no sigils.

The life I'd hoped for seemed impossible, and grief consumed me for not just tonight, but every night after. Heg stayed by my side, offering her support with gentle pressure. I sniffed, blinked back my tears, and let a wave of numbness wash over me. Harol squeezed my hand before going to the others.

Crysul, Renn, and a dozen fresh guards with their familiars surrounded a body. Prince Drevan stood off to the side consulting his own entourage of guards. I forced myself to my feet, ignoring the dizzy tilt of my head and the wave of pain swaying my stomach.

Harol clamped onto Rhofe's shoulder, and another guard clutched Alfy. Confusion muddled my mind. If the royals were alive, who was important enough to gain everyone's attention?

"The marking?" Crysul demanded.

I stumbled closer. The body was a mercenary, but I didn't remember anything special about him. They hadn't seemed to have a leader. A guard reached down and plucked something from inside his shirt.

Crysul turned to me. "Brin, is the last attacker dead?"

"He…t-they—"

"Spit it out."

My chin fell. "One soldier and his wolf familiar escaped, My Queen. I did my best, but—"

"You failed your fellow handmaidens. You failed to capture the remaining enemies. And now this?" Crysul held up a knife.

My brows furrowed. It was a handmaiden's knife. Black, thin, and etched with a honey badger emblem on the hilt. Cold terror flooded my chest, and I took a step back.

Fucking fucker! Heg seethed. *Let me Surge, Brin. I swear I can get us across the bridge!*

I held back the spell, my heart breaking in two. All Heg wanted to do was protect me, and I her. But we'd never make it across the bridge. Not injured and spent as we were.

"I have no knives," I said, showing my sleeves. My balance wavered, and I wobbled. "You'll find three more strewn somewhere in this mess."

"Ah, yes, but this one is special." Crysul hardened her gaze. My heart stopped as an understanding passed between us. The dagger didn't matter; this was revenge for Rhofe hurting Jekell, and for me giving her the means to do so. "Your dagger was found untarnished by blood, inside the clothes of an attacker. Seize her! Lock up her beast!"

"No!" I screamed, yanking my arms away from the soldiers. Heg yowled, and someone ripped her away. "Don't hurt her! Please, don't hurt her! We didn't do anything wrong!"

They didn't relent. I whipped my head around, searching for Drevan. His familiar saved me once. Maybe I could plead for mercy.

The prince leaned against one of the half-crumbled pillars. Arms crossed, silently watching.

"Prince Drevan, I swear this was not my doing!" I pleaded. "If you find the one that got away, you'll see I had nothing to do with it!"

"The prince has a wedding to prepare for," Renn snapped. Medge was cradled in his arms, not moving, but the king didn't look distraught enough for his familiar to be dead. "Sadary brought their enemies here. They poisoned the minds of our subjects and turned them against us, but make no mistake, this alliance will be forged. My daughter will make her vows, and the prince's signet will be on new treaties by sunrise. Take this traitor to the dungeons."

I thrashed against the four guards dragging me away. Black blurred the edges of my vision, and my heartbeat pounded in my ears. Only mine.

Heg! I cried into the void. Without a response to soothe my despair, I fought as hard as my weakening body would allow.

Rhofe bowed her head, and Harol wouldn't watch, while Drevan looked on with cautious curiosity. Crysul's cruel smirk burned into my memory.

I tried to convince myself they'd trapped my familiar in a Containing Box. Yes, she was only behind a spell.

She's not dead. She's not dead. She's not dead, I told myself as my body finally gave out.

⬥◇⬥

Someone ripped off my cowl.

"Won't be needing this, will you?" a man spat, wet flecks landing on my cheek. I swayed, but the restraints clamping my hands behind my back prevented me from falling.

A second man pinched my face. "Pretty little thing. Bet you'd look better without all those clothes."

I glared from under my lashes. "You think the handmaidens were only for show? You don't scare me."

"No?" The soldier's hand dipped down and squeezed a breast. "There are a thousand ways to taste you and never leave a trace."

The clang of a distant door caused both soldiers to jump. The first threw my headdress at my feet before they both hurried back to their posts.

With the most immediate threat gone, I studied my surroundings. Three stone walls and one grid of slimy steel bars cased me in. A torch just out of sight cast a soft orange glow on the dirty straw and gave enough light to see the cell across from mine was empty.

I tried to wrench my arms to test my restraints, but my hands had been thrust into a brick behind me. A spell caused the stone to encase my arms up to my elbows. I couldn't move my hands—could barely feel them, actually. Pins and needles numbed all the way up to my shoulders.

I shivered. The wet blood soaking my leg and side chilled my skin but did nothing to alleviate the fevered burn heating the wounds. A dull pain pulsed through me with every breath.

"So, this is the reward for loyalty?" a familiar voice drawled. Prince Drevan stepped out of the shadows and stopped in front of my cell.

"You should be celebrating. It's the eve of your wedding," I said with as much energy as I had, which was none.

Drevan's lips lifted in a half smile. "Tell me, are the hand-maidens really whores, or was that a story you spun up?"

"We're useful. Sometimes the job takes us to a bed." I waited for his face to twist with disgust, but the orange haze hid his reaction. I had no shame in the subject, and his opinion didn't matter.

"Sadary is known for our warriors, but Hillcrest is known for more than their gold," Drevan said. "There are rumors of what it takes to live in a castle. Tell me, how did you end up as the princess's protector?"

"Why should I?" Fear soured to anger, which sharpened my tongue.

The prince reached for his pocket and extracted a key. I tried to step away as the bars creaked open, but my hands restrained the movement.

"I know you're innocent." He took a step forward. And another.

I straightened my shoulders and raised my head. "Oh? Suddenly feeling charitable? You could have spoken up on the terrace."

Drevan's dark eyes studied mine. Without Heg to help with my vision, his features were slightly blurred. I flinched as he lifted his hand, but he only tucked a stray hair behind my ear. "I know you're innocent, because I hired those mercenaries."

"What?" I whispered.

Alic. Taalyn. The girl in the kitchens. *Heg.*

I strained forward and slammed my forehead into his nose. "Motherfucker!"

Drevan stepped out of range and wiped his bleeding nose with the back of his hand.

"Guards!" I shouted.

A low chuckle rumbled in his chest. "You think the words of the accused hold weight? Pointing the blame on someone else means nothing. If you answer my questions, I won't let them kill you. No promises on your familiar, though."

"You little shit," I seethed.

"Oh, I'm sorry. I'm supposed to marry some girl I've never met, bring her into an active military operation, and leave her to her own devices while I lead my men?" Drevan crossed his arms. "I need an heir, and I won't abandon my children in the hands of someone who can't defend them."

"So, you thought you'd test Rhofe? People died tonight, Drevan. The handmaidens. Guards. Childr—" My voice broke, and a tremor ran through my lip.

"Five handmaidens died. One survived, and the princess is alive. I'd say it was a success, more or less."

We weren't people to him, just pawns. My spirit crushed with the weight of defeat. "What do you want?" I asked dully.

"If I'm to take a bride from Hillcrest, I want to understand the workings of this court. How did you get here? How do your people survive the mist?"

I swallowed. My story didn't matter much in the grand scheme. If answers would get him to leave, I'd tell him what he wanted to know. "I was born the first of three children at the base of the mountain. My father worked as an overseer in the mines, and my mother helped in the refinery. There are officials at a waypoint between the castle and the mines. We call them Sifters."

Green-tinted memories floated through my mind, but everything was fuzzy. It was only five years ago, but I could barely remember my home.

I cleared my throat and continued, "If you have enough talent, the Sifters will grant you a probationary period in the castle. Imagine fighting for your life by mastering etiquette and how to chop vegetables."

"Imagine fighting for your life on real battlefields," Drevan countered.

"You think becoming a handmaiden was easy?" I snarled. An ache pounded in my shoulders from the movement. "My father took me under his wing instead of my mother. A girl of ten working alongside grown men. He taught me strength and endurance, but the mist weakened my eyesight and damaged my circulation. I can't fucking feel my arms right now. My hips and legs will go numb soon, and my feet are freezing."

Drevan frowned.

I threw my head back and scoffed. Cold feet was what bothered him?

"Can you see me?" he asked in a gentle tone.

I squinted with a mocking tilt to my head. "Yes, you idiot. I'm not blind. Everything's a bit blurry, that's all."

Drevan picked up my headdress and dusted it off. He paused over the slit matching the slice on my cheek. "So…what? You muscled your way into a position here?"

"I was able to hide my poor eyesight by sense sharing, but the Sifters still denied me. I couldn't wash bedding properly. I mean, who had bedding to wash when you were barely surviving? My parents scraped together everything they had to bribe one of the Sifters. I spent two years scrambling to become a handmaiden and the last three trying to keep it that way." A giggle bubbled out of me. "All for it to come crashing down in one night."

"There was something else," Drevan said, mulling over his words before continuing. "Why would your queen pin the attack on a handmaiden instead of having you remain at her daughter's side?"

"Have you considered Crysul knows you did it and wants you to sign the goddamn treaties anyway?" She probably didn't, and Hillcrest was too desperate to refuse if she did, but I wasn't about to explain her history with Rhofe. It was a weakness he'd most likely press, and I didn't want the princess in the middle more than she already was.

"Feisty, aren't you?" Drevan chuckled. "You're covering for her. Why? She'll order your execution soon enough."

"The royals aren't so wasteful," I said. "They'll kill my familiar and send me to the mines. Maybe my father will be my keeper." I huffed at the sick twist of irony.

Drevan tilted his head. "Even knowing your fate, you're still loyal."

"I lost everything tonight, and you took that from me."

The prince tugged my cowl back on and adjusted the fabric. As much as I hated to admit it, the gesture was a kindness. I felt more myself with the covering.

"Sometimes fire is needed to clear the way for a better future," he murmured. His fingers trailed over my uninjured cheek before he turned and left.

As time stretched on, my body became less and less usable. Sharp prickles consumed my arms and legs, and spikes of searing pain throbbed in my side and leg. It seemed the only detail I could focus on was my heartbeat, but it felt so lonely without Heg's.

There was no way to tell how long I'd be down here, which worsened as I floated in and out of a blurry trance. Exhaustion drowned my body, but sleep would not find me.

The creak of my cell door finally roused me from my delirium. I blinked and cringed away from the harsh torchlight. Had it been one hour? Two?

The guards had returned, and I as much as I tried to infuse energy into my limbs, it was no use. Rather than reach for my breasts, they grabbed behind me. Confusion muddled my mind as they released the spell in the brick and caught me as I toppled forward.

"On your feet, bitch," one growled.

"W–where…?"

"Muck like you doesn't deserve the air here," the other hissed.

My feet wouldn't respond when they hauled me up. When I fell again, they grabbed my arms and dragged me. A spiral staircase and several hallways later, they threw me to the floor, and my hands slapped cool marble.

One glance around the room had me wishing they'd take me back to the dungeon.

Chapter 5

Paintings and ceramic vases filled with gold-dipped flowers decorated the walls. Candles brightened the space, their shadows dancing as they flickered.

Crysul waited on a red velvet couch in front of me. Her face pinched with mild distaste at my presence. Jekell flexed his claws and glared from where he lay next to her.

Footsteps echoed a moment before the door slammed shut. Trying, and failing, to push myself to my feet, I managed to settle onto my knees with my hands splayed for balance.

The queen sipped a deep maroon wine from a crystal glass. "I should have dug out the infection when I first saw the signs. In truth, I didn't think my daughter would ever present a real challenge. Still don't."

I remained silent. Hate simmered below my skin, but they still had Heg.

"Rhofe was never going to win. You know that," Crysul said. "So, why were you so persistent in encouraging her insubordination?"

Candlelight caught on the glass, and I focused on the movement since the rest of her features were hidden in slight misfocus. "My role was to protect the princess. I was only doing my duty."

Glass shattered, and wine pooled between my fingers.

"None of the other handmaidens had an inkling to turn my kin against me," Crysul hissed. Her brow creased with indignation. "Do you think you're special? Do you think you're the only older sibling bribed into the castle to pave the way for the rest of the brood?"

It wasn't enough she had Heg. She'd go after my family, too? I clenched my jaw and became very aware I was in a room alone with the queen and her lion. One door behind me. Two small windows to my left, but there was probably a sizable drop on the other side, and I'd never be able to scale the wall in my condition.

A lost look crossed the queen's face. "You think I'm cruel and unfeeling. You turned my daughter against me for it, and I suppose I should have seen that coming. But how would you react if you bore a daughter and not a son? A son could stay and rule, while daughters are always destined to be sacrificed for the well-being of others."

Wine seeped in my cuticles, and I couldn't stop thinking about the blood that'd be prevented if I took the fall for a war Drevan started.

"What can a mother do except carve the affection out? How could I love her and let her go? She was the price to keep my people alive, and I did what I had to do to ensure Hillcrest's future, even if I had to mold her into a child too scared to stand up for herself." Crysul ran a soft hand over Jekell's head. "So, you see, I've destroyed the only child I have to save a kingdom going to die anyway."

My head snapped up. "What?"

Did tonight mean nothing? All the death for naught?

Crysul rose to her full height. "The prince has rejected my daughter's hand, and we have one chance—*one*—to mend this alliance."

Unease and nausea churned in my gut.

"You will share Prince Drevan's chamber tonight and wed him in the morning. Please him as a woman and a companion. Any defiance, any hint of rebellion, and your familiar will be punished."

Heg was alive. I blinked back tears as my throat tightened with relief. Everything would be okay. I could find a way to salvage this.

"Drevan has demanded your familiar come with you when you leave for Sadary, but make no mistake." Crysul pushed my shoulder with her foot. I was too feeble to resist, and my body rocked to the floor as I curled into myself. "Your brother and sister's fate are in your hands. They could have a nice life here. I'm in need of new guards and handmaidens, but the mines always need more workers. Your choice."

I squeezed my eyes shut and tucked my forehead against my knees. The guards returned, their rough hands dragging me to my feet and pulling me back through the hallways. My head was too dizzy to follow their path. A whoosh of cool air rushed past before the floor came up to meet me again.

"Brin!" Rhofe shouted.

I screwed my eyes shut and let out a weak moan.

"Get the fuck out!" the princess screamed. She wasn't talking to me, was she? "You! Do something!"

A chilled rag rubbed along my side and leg. I blinked up at an old woman, relaxing when I recognized Yelane, our resident witch. She wore a faded green dress and a belt with pouches to hold her ingredients.

Yelane had originally come from the covens in Alganise, traveling as some witches did. She might have been drawn here to study our familiars as she didn't have one of her own, but she didn't talk much.

"Hey, it's going to be okay," Rhofe whispered as Yelane snipped at the fabric around my wounds.

I lay on the floor in the princess's chambers, my mind replaying the conversation with Crysul and the events of tonight over and over. Not with panicked fervor, but with defeated acceptance. It'd taken me months to prepare for all the what ifs of my escape. How was I supposed to manage it now? Or had fate given me another path?

Rhofe swiped the cloth over my wounds again as Yelane prepared a needle and thread. Clutching the princess's hand, I tried to stay as still as possible at the first bite of the stitches. In… Out… In… Out…

Rhofe stayed by my side until Yelane finished with the needle and smeared a healing balm over my ribs, thigh, and cheek. Her spells didn't completely heal them, but the worst of the pain was gone as well as the heat of infection.

"I'm so sorry," Rhofe whispered when she left.

I held my breath as I pushed to a sitting position. "Failing to kill Jekell only angered your mother. You should have neutralized the threat."

"I'm sorry, okay?" Rhofe cried. "I'm not like you. I'm not strong. I can't focus when Alfy is in danger."

"Then you'll always be subject to your mother's rule," I said. Maybe I shouldn't be angry with her, but I simply couldn't bring myself to care. I'd given her a chance to protect Alfy, and she hadn't had the courage to take it. What kind of person let their familiar be hurt…or taken? What kind of person was I if I lived and Heg didn't?

Rhofe recoiled with tears falling down her face.

"Why are you crying?"

"Your words were cruel." Rhofe sniffed.

I leaned forward with bitterness filling my heart. "There's not a scratch on your pretty skin. You didn't get thrown into a cold dungeon, and you don't have to bed the prince or marry him, for that matter. Stop pretending your troubles compare to anyone else's, especially your people."

Rhofe's face scrunched with an indignant scowl, and she tugged off my headdress. "At least fate gave you a mate."

"What?" My hands flew to my hair and mussed it so I could see the strands.

Rhofe went to the vanity and tossed a handheld mirror in my lap. "You have nothing to complain about either. He's going to take you away and give you a happy life."

There it was—a streak of dark black in my light brown hair. *Fuck.* My heart stuttered. How? When? I flipped through memories of Prince Drevan. He hadn't had it on the terrace. The dungeons? Maybe… It was dark. I couldn't really see.

Hope sparked in my heart, chasing away the dark thoughts circling my mind. I'd scoffed at Rhofe's faith, but maybe fate was giving me a second chance.

Rhofe held up the red dress she'd wanted to wear. "You have the confidence I would have never had to pull it off," she mumbled. "Let's get you bathed."

With a mix of anticipation and anxiety, I let her tug me up and fill a tub. Being Drevan's fated mate would probably save me, but Heg could still be used against me. I needed to find her.

My mind raced, mentally pathing the castle in a search grid, but there were too many dangers. The guards could subdue me right outside the door. I could climb out the window, but would my leg hold my weight? Even if I managed to find Heg, what was to say someone didn't kill her before I got to her?

No, I wouldn't be able to win blinded by anger and desperation.

Rhofe chatted the whole time she braided my hair, listing all the ways my future would make a turn for the better. I'd get to decorate a big ballroom, tour local orchards, maybe even have a romantic sunset kiss with my one true love.

I almost let myself believe the dream. In the first year as a handmaiden, an ambassador had brought the royals peaches and honey as a gift. I hadn't been able to taste them, but seeing the drips of amber over the rich marigold slices was perhaps the first moment in my life I knew there was a future out there for me. One with peaches and honey and an orchard with clear skies and fresh air.

If fate was kind enough to give me a mate, maybe it'd also let me taste such a delicacy, but the hole in my chest wouldn't let me fully believe. Never mind Drevan's hand in destroying my escape, but a future without Heg was no future at all.

Rhofe stood me up like a doll and draped the dress over me. The fabric was a thick, luxurious silk with long lace sleeves. The bodice dipped low, and two slits ran up the sides.

A deep well of sadness tightened my throat. Tears stung my eyes, and I blinked them back with a tired sigh.

I wanted to curl up with Heg under my mother's quilt like I used to when I was young, but I was all grown up. No one was going to protect us but me. And right now, protecting us meant burrowing my fear so deep no one could see it.

Crysul could force my hand, but she'd never earn my loyalty. Drevan could take my body, but he'd never have my spirit.

"Clip the sleeves," I whispered.

Rhofe frowned. "Do you really want to? You won't be wearing much, and your scars will show. Granted, they're not that big, but—"

"Drevan will respect them. They're a show of strength." And frankly, I didn't give a shit. I liked my scars, and everything I'd been through wasn't for me to be reduced to a bargaining chip.

A small sense of relief lifted from my chest when the fabric ripped. Rhofe stepped back, the torn sleeves dangling in her hand. She swallowed and looked away. "I suppose this is goodbye."

I reached out a finger and tapped her temple. "Forge your own fate."

She nodded and looked out the window as I left. Four guards surrounded me and led me to the guest wing. My posture slipped from calculated alertness into a walk of mastered grace, and I was grateful my wounds didn't hinder my performance.

I had no weapons, no magic, and no Heg. And yet, when we reached the prince's room, my breathing was deep, and my mind was clear as I pushed the door open.

Chapter 6

"If I wanted a painted doll, I'd have accepted the princess's hand." Drevan lounged in a chair, the low fire casting dark shadows across his form. Even if my heart denied it, my eyes couldn't help but find the brown streak in his black curls.

I didn't feel any different from this morning besides all the aches and pains, but maybe the stories got it wrong. They said being mated intensified a hum of magic in one's heart. Maybe with Heg gone, it'd messed it all up.

I tilted my head, pretending to watch the guards close the door behind me, but used the opportunity to scan the room. Drevan's quarters were dominated by a massive four-poster bed draped with thick gold fabric. There was a trunk at the end of the footboard, but it was too small to use to climb into the rafters. There was no escape up, anyway. The prince's window was tightly shut, and thin streams of moonlight mocked me from the safety of the sky.

I relaxed my weight into my hip and crossed my arms. "I'm whatever you want me to be."

Drevan scoffed and brought a chalice to his lips. "I've no interest in your masks."

"What about a puppet?" I countered, stepping forward. "*Take the fall, Brin. Be my whore, Brin.* You're no better than them."

Drevan discarded the cup and rose to meet me. His jaw worked back and forth while his chest heaved. "It wasn't me who asked you to present yourself half-naked. And for the record, my wife will not be a whore. She will always have a choice."

I scoffed. "A choice? In what? They have my familiar, and soon enough Heg will be passed to you. There's no choice in that."

Drevan's frown deepened, and he pointed to the little tray on the windowsill. "Eat," he said, before sweeping out of the room.

The silence in his wake amplified the loss of Heg's heartbeat in my chest. My shoulders trembled, so I strode to the other side of the room to distract myself from tumbling into a pit of despair. My frayed emotions could only handle so much.

Little crackers with dollops of smoked fish were arranged on the tray. Some of them had a piece of cheese with a bit of berry spread instead. I took half a bite and chomped down three more. Fish and fruit were delicacies I hadn't had the chance to indulge in before.

I swallowed, and the small comfort lost all its luster when I realized the food wasn't hot. The kitchens weren't in working order yet—there was no one to cook. Drevan had probably used rations he'd packed with him. My jaw clenched.

The little girl's death was on Drevan as much as it was on me. But not only hers, the handmaidens' as well. Yes, circumstances raised tensions between us, but underneath we were all connected with a sad sort of comradery…and now I was the only one left.

Was this the life I'd find outside of Hillcrest? War and blood?

No. I refused to believe every kingdom was ruled by survival. I was getting out of here, and when I did, I wouldn't stop until I found a life worth living.

Raised voices rang out in the hallway a moment before Drevan opened the door and shoved Crysul through. She sprawled on the rug in a position I'd been in not too long ago.

I reached for my knives and found bare skin. Instinct had me adjusting for hand combat, but I forced myself to slink to the edge of the bed with an innocent look of confusion. As much as I reveled in standing over Crysul's trembling form, she'd turn her anger on her subjects when we were gone.

"Care to explain?" I raised an eyebrow at Drevan. My breath hitched when I caught the black box under his arm.

He kept his seething gaze on the queen as he set the box on the bed. "My future wife will not be treated as a common traitor. Her familiar belongs to no one but her."

I couldn't hold myself back any longer. Snatching the box and holding it close to my chest, I backed away from them, intentionally angling towards the window.

"I believe you have something to say." Drevan prompted her with his toe.

The queen's hair was mussed, and she looked distraught without her familiar. Where was Jekell? Did Drevan kill him? For some reason, the thought bothered me. With Medge injured, I doubted Renn put up much of a fight beyond a few choice words. I didn't like seeing Hillcrest as weak, and I didn't want Drevan getting any ideas about taking over.

Crysul straightened her posture as best she could while kneeling on the floor. "Your loyalty has been invaluable to the integrity of this kingdom. However, I hereby release you, Brin Minedaughter, from your servitude."

I almost snorted. Servitude? I was not a slave, even if she wished to label me as such. Minedaughter was a slur Drevan wasn't knowledgeable enough to pick up on. The queen pinned me with a look, saying everything she needed to without words.

This was a show for the Prince of Sadary to feel powerful. If it wasn't Heg, she'd threaten my family, and if it wasn't my family, she'd go after little girls I'd see my sister in. Drevan could throw his muscle around, but women learned long ago to wage war in silence.

I hugged the box closer. A tiny part of me wanted to sink to my knees. My energy was long spent, and I had somehow managed to find myself in the protective arms of a fated mate. I could let someone else shield me for once.

And yet…

The color of my hair didn't dictate my character or inflate my arrogance. Yes, my parents bribed my way into the castle, but I was the one who survived until that happened. I was the one who kept my place among my ever-changing peers. So, Mated Brin would not cast away Minedaughter Brin, especially not for a man.

Drevan waited for my answer, his face displaying a calculated evenness with a hint of anticipation. Did he think this pleased me? Seeing the queen in a humbling state was a temporary balm to the many wounds stripped over my heart.

I could have smashed her fingers. Could have cut her face and left her a blubbering mess, but I was not cruel. I was not her.

"The terms of the agreement will be amended once more." I lifted my chin. "Twelve handmaidens will be taken from the base of the mountain, not six. Choose second and third daughters. Make sure my sister is among them, and my brother is chosen to train as a guard."

The queen slid her gaze to Drevan, and he gave her a curt nod. She pursed her lips. "It seems I will need to arrange a messenger."

"Tonight, Crysul," I pressed. "You have one chance to mend your mistakes."

The slightest sense of understanding rippled through the queen as Drevan hauled her up and shoved her into the arms of his guards in the hallway. My words didn't mean much to the prince, but they directly tied my actions to the queen's, and she knew she had no choice but to fulfill my request if she wanted me to play my part.

"You don't trust her?" Drevan asked. "She'll do as I say if she hopes to maintain an alliance."

But I didn't know how this night would go, did I? I didn't know if he'd use me and toss me to the side. My siblings wouldn't be safe near the queen, but they weren't safe down with the mist and the mines, either. At least this way they would have a full belly.

Rather than answer Drevan, I snatched the dull knife used for spreading the jam and sank to the floor with the box. The preserve tasted tart on its own as I cleaned the blade with a swipe of my tongue. Jamming it into the crack of the wooden planks marked with witch runes, I wrenched at it to weaken the joints.

The soft metal knife bent under the pressure, and a low hum of frustration thrummed in my throat. Flipping the handle, I banged at the top of the box, each stroke more angered and less effective.

"May I?" Drevan extended his hand for the box.

"I've got it," I bit out. A little wood wouldn't deter me, even if it was enchanted. Shoving the knife deeper, I widened the crack in the corner.

"Let me help," he insisted.

With a huff, I shoved my sore fingers between the planks and pulled as hard as I could. The wood snapped back—right onto my fingers. I dropped the box with a hiss.

Drevan went to pick it up, and anger got the best of me. I reached for his whip and cracked it by his heels. Metal screeched against stone, tearing at my ears.

"I said I have it," I growled.

Drevan raised his hands, the ghost of a smile lifting his lips as he backed up.

"Is this a joke to you?" I snapped. "Because this is never going to work if you don't respect me."

Drevan's eyes drifted down. I thought he was looking his fill at my heaving chest, but when I glanced at my hand, I dropped the whip and swiped the box up. Seemingly melting out of the metal was a black cobra. Wisps of shadow turned into shiny scales, and the snake wound up Drevan's body until it rested over his shoulders.

"This is Sembri," he said, picking his whip up from the ground. Reflected flames from the hearth danced on the sharp metal sections as if nothing had happened.

"How?" My eyes darted between the snake and the whip, unable to understand how one had become two. Such a spell hadn't been used in Hillcrest, at least to my knowledge. An uneasy feeling spread through me. How much did I not know?

"War changes people." Drevan trailed a finger over the crest of Simbri's head. She preened at the attention. "You learn to keep things you value safely tucked away. Hillcrest is all stone and metal. Sadary? We built fortresses, yes, but also gardens and stables and all sorts of marvelous wonders. You'd be safe there. Happy, even."

"Until one day your enemies come to haunt you." I tightened my grip on the box. "My cheek will be pressed into a pool of my children's blood while the men you've gloated over will take their pound of flesh. What happens then, hmm?"

Drevan's eyes darkened. "And what of your future here? I'm offering you a lifetime of happiness with the slight possibility of demise. You have no future here. If it wasn't for me, you'd still be down in that cell."

I narrowed my eyes. "If it wasn't for you, I wouldn't have been in that cell in the first place."

Drevan ran a hand through his hair with a frustrated huff, and his jaw ticked. After a beat of tense silence, he stalked out the door for the second time.

Chapter 7

Fucking princes and their fucking egos, I grumbled to myself. Setting the box down again, I hammered away at the weakened corner.

Drevan came back and dropped a packed bag and a chisel before returning to his seat to nurse his sour mood. Sembri was nowhere to be seen, so I assumed she'd gone back into the whip.

"Thank you," I murmured. I was reluctant to give him any grace, but besides murdering the castle staff, he'd been relatively kind.

"You'd have a good life with me," he said as an intense wanting simmered in his eyes. He needed me to trust him, to surrender my future and let him whisk me away to a better life.

And maybe he was right. I had no future here. My hopes of escaping into a blissful countryside were dashed the moment he'd set his sights on Hillcrest.

A pit of guilt writhed in my belly. I could take care of myself. Shit, I'd been doing fine all these years. Not great, but no one truly thrived here.

I couldn't abandon my brother and sister while I picked flowers and danced in frilly dresses. My parents had tried the best they could, but it wasn't about them. They'd lived their lives and accepted their lot. Leaving had given me a sliver of hope I'd be able to pull my siblings out along with me. No more burning mist. No more scrappy fights for trash thrown down the mountain.

In my mind, they were still the same little kids looking up to me with wide eyes and tear-streaked faces before I'd left for the castle. They were older now, probably working in the mines alongside my dad.

Crysul would take them under her wing. Use them, maybe even turn them against me, but what choice did I have? Here, they might see the same ambassadors I did. Maybe think to themselves to pack a bag and cross the bridge on their own.

My fingers trembled as I once again shoved them between the planks and strained against the wood. The planks snapped back and smashed my fingers between them. Letting out a frustrated growl, I renewed my efforts with the chisel.

Drevan didn't say anything, and I found myself appreciating his calm demeanor while I took out my anger on the damn box.

Even with the little options life had given me, I'd still found a way to make my own choices. Mentoring Rhofe against her mother. Weaseling my way into servant positions to eavesdrop on business meetings with the other kingdoms. Lingering too long where I shouldn't to glance at maps or inventory lists or anything else mildly useful.

And now a streak of hair and a faraway prince were taking it all away. I needed a little win. Just something, anything, to go my way. I needed my Heg.

Letting out a harsh scream, I threw the chisel at the door. It clattered to the floor.

Drevan adjusted in his seat. "May I please help?"

I waved my hand dismissively and paced. My heart pounded in my ears, and even though my fingers stung, I ran them through my hair and pulled the strands tight. The pricks of pain helped ground me. Helped me focus on that instead of the heartbeat missing from mine.

"I had a bag packed for you if you'd like to change. You seem like the type of girl to prefer function over fashion." Drevan swiped the chisel and knelt by the box. His muscles rippled as he worked at the same corner I had, but his movements were steadier, less panicked and frantic.

His back was to me for the moment, so I grabbed the bag and was surprised to see my handmaiden uniform, but there were no weapons. "Do you see me as a threat, or as a woman who shouldn't worry about such things?"

Drevan chuckled. "In my kingdom, women fight just the same as men. I didn't want you to get any bright ideas. I happen to like my guards."

"I want to be armed when we leave," I replied.

"As you wish."

It made me feel a bit better, but not much. I changed and braided my hair, but kept my headdress and boots off.

CRACK.

I rushed to Drevan as he yanked the top boards off. Inside the box, Heg lay on her back, unmoving. Her head lolled to the side, her fur crusted with thick, dried blood. I swept her into my arms, cradling her tight. A faint heartbeat seconded mine, and my throat tightened as tears dripped from my chin.

"I have a healer kit," Drevan said, rifling through one of his bags.

I nodded, unable to speak. *Heg?*

No answer. Not even a flutter of her eyelids.

I kissed her brow and rocked her gently.

"Here, let me take a look," the prince said.

"I've got it."

Drevan handed me a small pouch, and I set Heg on the bed to assess her wounds. The bite marks on her neck and the gash behind her ear needed stitches, while the punctures along her belly needed healing ointment. While I worked, a sense of calm settled over me. My hands steadied, and my sutures became more even.

Worry for my future nibbled at the back of my mind, but Heg was here, and everything would be okay. Once she was bandaged, I settled her in the crook of my arm and swayed next to the fire.

"Why is she not waking up?" Drevan asked, his voice laced with concern.

"The Containing Box lulled her to a deep sleep. She might not wake for some time," I said. He frowned, and I raised an eyebrow. "Surely you have boxes in Sadary?"

Drevan shook his head. "We don't keep prisoners for long, and if we do, we don't keep their familiars alive."

I huffed out a humorless laugh. "Sometimes their death would be preferred. When we're young, our parents tell us to behave, or the guards will box your familiar. Not dead, just asleep. Giving you a thread of hope to keep you in line to maybe one day earn enough favor to get them back."

"I…did not know." Drevan's hand drifted to his whip, stroking it the same as he did Sembri's head. "Why do they do that?"

I waved at the room around us. "Smell the air. It doesn't burn your lungs. Sting your eyes. The people down there outnumber us a thousand to one. What better way to keep them in check than to take away their familiars?"

Drevan kicked the box to the far corner. "You don't need to worry about that anymore. Your familiar is your own. I'd never use her against you."

I didn't believe him, but his words were sweet. Heg yawned, and a smile flickered across my face. She snuggled closer as I trailed a finger over her cheek. I still didn't feel the influx of magic I was supposed to, but I'd worry about that later.

"It's late. Would you like to go to bed?" Drevan extended a hand in invitation.

I followed his gaze, and dread bloomed in my gut.

"I won't touch you tonight, not unless you want me to," he reassured me. "Or any night, for that matter."

Again, his words soothed me, made me put down my guard, and I didn't know what to do. If he was putting on a show, he was doing a good job of it, but if this was truly his real self, then he'd be saying the same things.

Drevan waited, not moving until I did.

With a defeated sigh, I pulled back the covers and curled into Heg as close to the edge as I could. Drevan took off his boots, set his whip next to the bed, and climbed in after me. At least he respected my space and kept to his side.

"I'm a good man, Brin. I'll be a good mate, too."

I stroked the white stripe along Heg's head while I mulled over my response. "You might be a good man to some, but you're also a man of violence. How long until it's turned on me? Or worse, our children?"

A long beat of silence stretched between us. Drevan scrubbed his face and ran a hand through his hair. "I suppose there's no way to tell you, but I'm willing to show you each and every day, until you know in your heart you can trust me."

My lips from curved into a smile. Perhaps he was a good man after all, and our circumstances had shown his worst at the very start.

"What do you know of fated mates?" I looked over at him and tucked a hand under my cheek. Heg squirmed in her sleep, perturbed I'd moved us.

"Not much past the stories," Drevan admitted. "Sadary hasn't had a pair since the last time of peace, and they say there won't be another until there's peace once more."

"And you believe that?"

Drevan shrugged. "Doesn't matter what I believe. I don't win battles; my people do. If they believe there can be peace, there's hope for it to come."

My mouth tasted of ash. "So, I'm just a trophy you're going to tote around for your own benefit. You need me to rally your people, not because you see a future with me."

"Hillcrest is tied to Sadary now. Our enemies are yours, our allies your friends. If there is peace in Sadary, there is peace for Hillcrest. Besides, I came here looking for a partner I could build a life with."

My sister's wobbling lip flashed in my eye. "You also came for gold to fund your wars. If not for battles, then what use do you have of it?"

"We've been at war since my father was a child, and his father was a child, and many other fathers before them. My people tire of war, yet they can't hope for a life without it. We need the gold to gain victory over our adversaries or rebuild what we've lost."

My thoughts were too fast to follow and too many to keep track of, but my face remained pleasantly blank. Nodding, I said, "It's been a long night, and you've given me much to think about."

"Goodnight," he said in a low voice as he turned away.

The fire burned to glowing embers, and still, I did not sleep. My mind whirled, trying to piece to together a plan. Every outcome. Every choice. Like rearranging a maze with only chunks of segments, and every time I thought I had a way forward something stopped me in my tracks.

Not only did Hillcrest rely on me to maintain an alliance with Sadary for open trade with Vadril, but now Sadary relied on me to bring them peace with Oppanuk. Oh, and my siblings were also collateral damage caught in Crysul's web.

And me? My fate was to fuck and frolic.

It was probably vain and unimportant in the grand scheme of keeping two kingdoms whole, but the image of Rhofe biting into a peach kept replaying in my mind. Bright sunlight had gleamed through the liquid gold as she'd swirled the honey stick and passed it over the fruit.

Heg smacked her tongue on the roof of her mouth and licked her jowl. *Mmh, honey.*

I gasped and hugged her close. *You're awake! How do you feel?* A flood of aches and pains twinged across my body. I kissed her on the brow. *It's going to be okay. We're going to Sadary tomorrow, and this will all be behind us.*

Sadness filled Heg's eyes when she blinked them open. *Will it?*

My response stuck on my tongue. I couldn't lie to Heg, not really. She was part of me, but it seemed lying to myself was much easier.

Hillcrest and Sadary are two sides of the same coin, I said, after taking a moment to form my thoughts. *I don't know what to do, and until I have a plan, I don't want to act rashly and mess up my chance when I do have one.*

What does your heart say? Heg asked.

I smiled. *I don't know. What do you say?*

She batted me with a paw. *That's not what I meant.*

I glanced at Drevan's sleeping form, then the window, and told her about everything that had happened since the terrace. Heg listened and watched the memories as they flowed between us.

I don't want to abandon my brother and sister by going to Sadary, I said. *And I'm scared they're going to get hurt if we get caught escaping.*

Heg licked the salt from my cheek. *How are you going to help them if you're not sure of your own future? We need to take care of ourselves first.*

I played with her paw. *What happens if I accidentally plunge Hillcrest into a war with Sadary? I mean, they'll be in the castle if Crysul upholds her end of the deal, but this'll be the first place Sadary will hit if there's a battle. I have to play my part for now.*

Heg nipped at my neck. *When have you ever given up? We had no future here, and you blazed ahead anyways to give us one. This man killed people for a test. A test, Brin. He doesn't deserve your effort, and he sure as shit doesn't deserve your heart.*

Her words echoed in my head, and a great sadness weighed my soul. New tears fell, but I dabbed them away with my sleeve.

Drevan would protect me…from enemies of his own creation. He'd give me a castle I couldn't leave. My summer afternoons would be filled with bright sunshine and gentle breezes, but I'd share his bed and bear his children. He'd give me a life every single person at the base of the mountain would kill for, and here I was looking at all the ways it fell short.

Taking a deep breath, I boxed all my buzzing thoughts and tucked them into the farthest corner of my mind. The only path now was forward.

Chapter 8

Careful not to wake the prince, I rolled out of bed and slipped on my boots.

As far as luck would have it, my options were limited. The hallway wasn't an option. I didn't want to hurt anyone else or raise the alarm. Plus, the only weapon in here was Drevan's whip, and it had Sembri embedded into it, or whatever his spell was. My best defense was the chisel. I shoved the half-full tin of salmon in my bag for Heg and swiped the jam and crackers for myself.

Climbing onto the sill and easing the window open, I glanced over to Drevan with a lingering look. Maybe once I was able to set up a life of my own, and get my siblings out of Hillcrest, I'd find him again. We were fated mates, right? Fate would bring us back together again.

Before I lost my nerve, I vaulted through the window and out onto the side of the castle. Heg's claws dug into my shoulder almost as much as my fingers clung to the bricks. Thankfully, my leg held. I wasn't a very good climber, but my hands knew the stone. My years at the castle hadn't worn away the years in the mines. Heg lent me her eyesight, so I was able to pick out the pieces jutting out the most, even in the pitch dark.

My toes jammed to the front of my boot as I scanned the wall to get my bearings. The guest wing sat below the floor reserved for Hillcrest elite and above the rooms for the rest of us. Small fires from the remaining braziers illuminated the Grand Terrace a few levels down to my right. Guards crawled over it. Whether to clean up or look for anything to help them track the remaining mercenary, I didn't know.

So much for stowing a bag, I grumbled.

We can't get to the cellar? Heg lifted her snout and sniffed.

I shimmied along a narrow ledge away from the terrace. Too many eyes. Heg dug her nose into the bag slung over my shoulder, and the strap slipped. My fingers strained to keep my torso close to the wall, but it was no use, and we tilted back.

"Heg!" I cried out.

She clung to my clothes, even when my side slammed into an sloped awning and we tumbled. The stone scraped my hands, and my fingernails ripped as I scrambled for purchase.

"Intruder!" a guard shouted.

Someone fisted my shirt through the arched opening, halting our descent, and yanked me into the hallway. I gasped, my heart stuttering.

"It's…Brin?" Harol turned to an older guard I didn't recognize for guidance. His osprey perched on his shoulder, not taking his eyes off us, and I couldn't find the second guard's familiar.

"She's trying to escape. Bring her to Crysul," the other man said.

"Not the prince?"

I swallowed. What if I killed Crysul? Then she couldn't hurt my brother or sister, and Rhofe would be rid of her, too.

I clenched my jaw and reached for the chisel behind my back. Going into the heart of the castle was a death sentence. Even I knew that.

"I'm sorry," I whispered.

Striking fast, I plunged the chisel into Harol's neck. His osprey screeched, clawing at my forearm while Heg launched from my shoulder. All three tumbled to the floor.

The older soldier had a moment to draw his sword, but I went low and punched out his knee. My leg strained with the movement, and my ribs pounded with my pulse. The soldier gasped and swung wildly.

I clicked my tongue twice while I backed away. Heg's ear flicked, and she scurried over to me on hearing alone.

The soldier now stood between us and the open arch, and he knew it. He didn't need to beat me, just wait for reinforcements. His lips moved, but I didn't hear him, and I wouldn't know when the other guards were coming, either.

Scuttles, Heg murmured.

Soldiers?

Scuttles.

I took another step back, scanning the floor, the walls—anything, everything.

A sly smile spread over the guard's face. I glanced behind me.

A dark red scorpion stood as tall as I was and blocked my only other means of escape. His stinger hung poised to strike.

A growl purred from Heg's chest. In one smooth motion, she took my body with a Surge and lunged. Pained tingles raced over my skin as Heg grew taller than me. As her jaws latched onto the scorpion's head, his stinger and claws struck my honey badger.

Poison coursed through our veins, a thick acid slowing Heg's movements. The soldier ran at me to subdue Heg, but she wasn't having any of it. Heg's teeth crunched through the scorpion's exoskeleton and with an angry whine, she threw his own familiar at him, smashing him into the wall. The scorpion's Surge withered with his injuries.

The soldier's mouth moved fast, but his words didn't deter my familiar. Heg released from her Surge as well, and as I flew into motion as she snapped up the soldier's familiar. With one last crunch, the scorpion disappeared down Heg's gullet.

The chisel left my hand and speared through the soldier's eye. I finished the job with a swift kick to the handle. The guard crumbled, and I wiped the chisel before bending for Heg. She jumped to my shoulder.

Cool air coursed into my heaving lungs as I climbed out onto the wall again. The guilt for killing them would come. Or maybe not, but there was no going back now.

My muscles quivered with exhaustion. The one thing keeping me focused on the next hold was Heg's heartbeat pounding in sync with mine. Determination and sheer will held me to the wall.

The scorpion's venom might have felled someone else, but honey badgers were immune to most poison, and living in the mist in my younger years had increased my natural ability to endure such things. Didn't mean it didn't burn like a bitch, though.

Beyond the pretty stone walkways Hillcrest visitors were escorted upon, piles of discarded rock were carved with unnatural overhangs and mounds of loose gravel to keep the villagers from climbing up. Stone was a poor way to keep miners away, but a visual safety made the castle folk feel better.

At least the majority of the rocks were to keep people out. Over the last few months, I'd covered for Heg as she'd mapped out a path to Dridgeton Bridge. A dozen guards were usually posted on each side of the bridge, but maybe there would be more after the attack?

My vision blurred as Heg took hers back and led me to the trail. We went slow, careful to avoid the gravel slides and the drop-offs. It wasn't quite morning yet, but the pitch black had lightened to a dark gray. A thrum of fear wound around my heart. What if we didn't make it?

I squashed the sting of doubt and sent the bee back to the box. No distractions. No doubts. No guilt until I was in a safe place to process.

Almost there, Heg reassured me.

We ducked behind a massive boulder, a throw away from the bridge.

Dridgeton Bridge was beautiful, if one could ignore its use to trap the people of Hillcrest. Moss grew in carved crevices, creating an intricate design of rich green. Torches lined the pathway and burned my night vision.

Blinking the yellow spots away, I assessed the area for weaknesses. A pair of towers stood on each end of the chasm. Dark green mist swallowed the depths and caressed the bottom of the bridge.

Over there, Heg said.

Following her nod, my stomach rolled at the faint trails of blood. The door of the near tower hung at an angle, and it'd swung in enough to see the pile of unmoving bodies thrown inside.

The mercenaries came across the bridge, I said. *We should make a run for it.*

But before I could step out, Heg's nose twitched, and she bared her teeth.

"It seems I underestimated you."

My heart sank. *No.*

Chapter 9

"You can come out," Drevan said. Pebbles crunched under his feet as he walked off the paved path. "I only want to talk."

There's no other way? I begged Heg.

Well, there's the u—

I can't do that. I clenched my jaw and grabbed the chisel. *I won't make it.*

Then we compromise. Heg looked up, absolute trust in her eyes.

I swallowed. Telling him about my siblings might secure them a trip to Sadary, but would he use them against me the same as Crysul?

"Before tonight, I had goals. Dreams. A family," I said, stepping out with my chin up. "I'm not going to give those up because you waltzed in with the promise of a good life."

Drevan stood before me, hands held out to show he was unarmed, but his whip was wrapped around his waist. I wasn't a fool.

"I don't expect you to, and I don't want you to," he said in a low voice. His calm demeanor soothed my bristles, but I didn't want it to.

Anger at my body's betrayal replaced the shallow tranquility. I let out an unbelieving exhale of desperation.

"Then let me go," I said, deciding to keep my siblings out of it. "A partner and children and all the heartwarming memories that come along with them sounds nice. I'm just not ready for all that yet. Let me come to you in my own time."

"I want that for you. Trust me, I do." Drevan walked a few steps away and settled his hands on his hips with a heavy sigh as he looked out across the bridge. "News of us will travel, and we'll both be targets. I can't keep you safe and let you go. Don't you see? I'll give you all the time in the world if you let me protect you."

"I'll shave my hair. Dye it, if that's too much of a giveaway." I crossed half the distance between us with slow steps. "Even if I don't want to, I'll resent you for the rest of my life if you do this. Take me, and you'll forfeit my heart. Let me go, and there's only a chance you'll lose me. I'm willing to take those odds."

Drevan turned to look at me, truly look at me. Did he see a woman who had fought for every scrap? Or a desperate girl begging for mercy? I knew which way I felt.

Heg brushed my calf, a challenge in her eyes as well.

"Have you ever been beyond Hillcrest's borders?" he asked.

I blinked. "What?'

"Have you left your home kingdom?"

"I don't see how that has anything to do with anything," I retorted.

"You don't know to watch for pickpockets in Alganise, or that they drug the food in Vadril to keep you coming back, or"—he stepped closer—"that flesh traders pose as innkeepers in Oppanuk. You are capable, you are strong, but the outside world is not where you want to get your sea legs. Let me show you my home. I'll even arrange a few trips if you'd like to travel."

His words turned bittersweet, and I'd had my fill.

I stared deep into his eyes, so he couldn't mistake the certainty in my voice. "I am capable of overcoming any obstacle in my way. Including you."

The part of me who'd entertained Rhofe and believed in a happy ending protested as my palms hit Drevan's shoulders, and I shoved him off the cliff.

Heg took off for the bridge with me on her heels. Air caught in my throat, and tears trailed down my cheeks as I tried not to think of what I'd done.

We were almost there. Ten steps… Five.

A black wall piled in front of us and coils of scales circled around and around. Some were so thick, I wouldn't have been able to wrap my arms around them. Sembri's hood billowed as she hissed a warning and blocked our way.

"You know, I really didn't want it to end like this, but you've given me no choice." Drevan strode towards us from behind, whip in hand.

Wait, how did he—

The snake, Heg growled. *She's too fast. Too big.*

The towers mocked us from behind Sembri, so close, and yet so far. We hadn't even made it onto the actual bridge.

I whirled on Drevan. "Let me go!"

I'd lost. He knew it, and I did, too, but it wasn't in my nature to give up. I just couldn't, and Heg rumbled in agreement.

I tried the last trick I had. Flipping the chisel, I pressed the tip to my neck. "One more step, I end this for both of us."

Drevan didn't even flinch. He flicked his wrist, and his whip knocked the chisel out of my hand. Heg, heart of my heart, did the only thing she could. My body froze over as she took it and swelled to match the cobra's size.

Sembri struck.

No! I screamed, but my voice was locked behind sealed lips. Pain burned into my shoulder and liquid fire poured into my veins from the cobra's venom.

"Give it up," Drevan said. His voice turned hard and unrelenting. "I don't want to hurt you."

Heg dug her claws into Sembri, even as the snake wrapped around her limbs and torso. My honey badger's teeth tore at flesh and bone while Sembri reared back, striking every time she lifted a paw.

"ENOUGH!" Drevan thundered.

Acid ate away at me from the inside out. My body was frozen, and I could do nothing but watch Heg and Sembri wrestle in an intertwined dance of death. Using her front paws to grab Sembri's head, Heg snarled and bashed the cobra's head into the ground. Again. And again. And again.

Drevan's fingers tightened, and he moved to raise his arm.

No! I cried. It was no use. My body wouldn't listen.

The metal whip sliced into Heg, cutting her from the back of the neck, across her belly, and over her hind leg. A burning hatred suffocated the sting from the venom, and only one thought consumed my mind.

Move.

Magic sang in my heart and thundered in my ears. My feet broke their frozen shell, and I barreled into Drevan with as much force as I could muster. This time, I clung to his shirt. This time, I tumbled over the edge with him.

Brin! Heg shouted.

Sembri hissed, but it was too late.

I held my breath as we dove into the mist. After a heartbeat of freefall, Drevan's back smashed into a boulder, and we tumbled onto a gravel mound. We didn't even have a chance to gain our footing before the gravel gave way and dumped us twenty more feet.

I tucked my arms close to my chest and kept my head down as we fell. The mist embraced me with its familiar bite. Itchy tingles raced over my skin, and my eyes blurred a bit more. This far down, the torchlight was faint, but I could make out Drevan and the shine of his whip between us once we'd rolled to a stop.

"You know." I coughed. "I really didn't want it to end like this, but you've given me no choice." The handle felt cool in my grasp as I picked the whip up and shuffled forward.

Drevan gasped, unable to do more than push to his knees and wheeze.

I might never find another partner. Might never have a family or feel the touch of a lover. Fate might even turn against me, but I didn't care. Only one bee had gotten out of the box.

Drevan's face had turned deep red, and little blisters had sprung on his hands. His body had no way to fight the mist, not even a little immunity like my people.

"I am strong, and capable of overcoming anything in my path," I repeated.

Understanding, and perhaps a touch of anger, overcame his features. When my arm arced, a line of blood spilled from his neck.

Someone should have warned the Prince of Sadary about the handmaidens of Hillcrest.

A wry smile twisted my lips before I fell to my knees and coughs wracked my lungs. Fumbling with my bag, I yanked out my headdress and pulled it over my head. The spell didn't work, but at least the fabric gave me some protection.

A waterfall of gravel pooled around my knees as Heg tumbled to a stop a few paces away. She'd given up the Surge, and her little chest heaved too fast for normal. I dragged myself over to her to pull her into my lap.

Can't go up, Heg murmured. *He had guards across the bridge. They're crossing to search now.*

A laugh bubbled out of me. Of course we couldn't go across the bridge. Of course after all that, I'd still be stuck in Hillcrest. Crysul would find another prince for Rhofe, I'd be sent to the mines, and Heg would go back in a box if we were lucky. I had no future, my siblings had no future, and I'd killed the only saving grace we'd had.

Heg pressed her paw weakly into my chest. *Strong.*

My back slumped against the gravel. I was exhausted, Heg was hurt, and still…I pushed to my feet and slung my bag across my chest so Heg could hold onto it. Stealing her vision, I picked my way farther down.

The gold in the castle was plated, not solid, and Dridgeton Bridge was no different. The underbelly was a network of decaying wood behind a thin layer of decorative stone, rotting from prolonged exposure to the mist. They had no order, just planks nailed together in a cross-hatched mess wherever the repairs needed to be.

Ripping my extra tunic, I wrapped Heg's new wounds as best I could and used the rest around my forearm where the osprey's talons had left deep gashes. I hadn't really felt them earlier, but now everything was catching up to me.

A heaviness weighed my bones, and my eyelids fluttered with exhaustion while the mist burned a track from my nostrils to my lungs, igniting sparks of fire in its path. My vision doubled, and I didn't know if it was a lingering effect from Sembri's venom, or the gas back to its old tricks.

You can do this, Heg murmured. She looked half-dead nestled in the bag slung across my chest, but at least she was alive.

My muscles protested as I stepped onto the first board and hoisted myself up. What didn't sting, ached and trembled. Still, I forced my body into a rhythm.

Hand. Hand. Foot. Foot.

Hand. Hand. Foot. Foot.

When my hands couldn't close any longer, I collapsed over a pair of sturdy boards and rested my cheek against the rough wood. The coughs had taken all I could give, and still a wheeze claimed my throat.

My forehead thudded into the plank with a choked sob after a glance. I'd only made it back up to the underside of the bridge. I still had to make the crossing over the gorge. Heg shuddered with a soft exhale, and her pulse weakened. I trailed a finger over her brow.

"I'm sorry," I whispered.

Heg's eyes closed in a slow blink. *So, that's it then?*

My lip wobbled like my sister's had all those years ago. *I'm so, so sorry. I can't make it.*

You help everyone. You give everything you have so others can better their lives. Heg's snout crinkled with anger. *And when you need your strength the most, you have none. Are you really going to let Rhofe fuss over her braids and eat peaches while you rot at the bottom of the mountain? Are you?*

Her anger became my own, flushing through my burning muscles. I bared my teeth. *Fuck that.*

A new sort of energy gave me the strength to lift my hand and grab another hold. It was jealous and full of hate, but my limbs kept moving. Half the boards cracked under my weight, and sometimes I had to climb almost up the stone or all the way down and swing with my legs dangling over the abyss.

My siblings deserved freedom, but dammit, so did I. I deserved the life I'd been fighting for.

Progress was hard-won, and I slipped more times than I thought survivable, but I kept moving. I did it tired. I did it with angry tears down my face, with every step feeling less rewarding than the last.

I looked over my shoulder again, then in front. I was only a dozen feet from the other side, and a few feet away from the safety of the rocky overhang below, but the boards here were too tightly nailed together. There wasn't a path to squeeze through.

With a weak cough, I inched my way to the side of the bridge. The outer stone here was cracked and revealed patches of nailed planks. The mist blurred my vision so much blinking hardly helped. Pressing my cheek against my bicep, I clung to a wide board and took a shuddering breath. I could do this.

Almost there, Heg encouraged.

As soon as she said it, the board beneath my boot jerked as a nail broke loose. I jumped to the next support without a plan, and not a moment later the plank cracked and disappeared into the void.

Off balance and with nothing but the tips of my toes balancing on a sliver of wood, I started to tip backwards. My nails scratched at a board almost out of reach, leaving bloody tracks in the grain as I searched for purchase.

Heg scrambled to help, looping the bag strap between her teeth and digging her claws into the board. The strap strained between us, the only lifeline anchoring me.

A calm sense of acceptance settled over me. I'd given my all and then some, but fate seemed intent on punishing me for my transgressions. My eyes closed as the mist embraced me, and my back dipped into the abyss.

Brin! Heg cried.

A ripple fluttered through my muscles, turning them to stone a moment before my ribs cracked from the impact of something heavy. Stone scraped along my forehead and upper arm as we collided with the rocky overhang.

Heg's back legs scraped the belly of the concave slope, and she dragged us both over the edge. I rolled to my side as warm prickles ran through my limbs. Heg lay an arm's length away with a heaving chest, busted sutures, fresh blood seeping into her fur. She must have jumped from the bridge with a Surge to catch me and used the momentum to get us to the other side.

I shuddered, my body too weak to do much else. *Thank you.*

Heg's ear flicked as she craned her head towards the mountain we'd come from. Torches bobbed near the far towers, with more making their way over the bridge.

Heg looked at me, and an understanding passed unspoken. She climbed onto unsteady feet. I pushed to my elbows, dragging my legs as I struggled to follow. My sight blurred as she took her vision into the rocks, and I collapsed with a choked sob. My throat was sore. My lungs ached.

As the minutes dragged on, I pressed my cheek against the cool stone and focused on the little gray pebbles in front of my nose. Eventually, curls of orange became brighter than the wisps of green. I blinked, lifting my head as much as I could.

Heg placed the torch in front of me and backed away. A heaviness pressed on my heart at the choice I needed to make. My fingers wrapped around the stick, and I used the side of a boulder to claw my way to my feet. With small, slow shuffles, I made my way to where the cluster of boards met the overhang.

The torch hovered a sliver away from the wood, and my arm wouldn't lower any more.

Word of Drevan's murder would reach his father. Sadary would come for me, and if they didn't find me, blame would be nailed on Hillcrest. Even if they caught me, Hillcrest still might suffer.

If I could delay the news by trapping Drevan's guards on the other side, I'd have a chance at slipping away, but burning the bridge would lock my siblings in a doomed kingdom. Hillcrest wouldn't have access to food or supplies without the bridge.

Leaving it standing would give the guards time to catch up to us.

Heg brushed against my calf. *You deserve a life, too.*

I know, I murmured.

And once we're settled, there's still a chance we could come back and get them. They're strong like you.

A tremor ran through my arm. The noble thing to do would be to lay down my life in hopes retribution would be sated with my sacrifice, but maybe all those years of telling myself I was fighting for my siblings was also partly to pursue a better future for myself without being burdened by selfish guilt. And now, I had no choice but to accept the truth or die with the lie.

I took a deep breath and lowered the torch. Flames licked at the dry wood, spreading over the bundle of boards in seconds. Tendrils of orange danced with swirls of dark green, and my mind quieted as if in reverence to my decision.

After a few moments, an icy tingle raced through my limbs. Heg nudged my side and helped me onto her back. I frowned as she turned to follow the ridge deeper into the mountains instead of to the road to Alganise.

I smelled a trail this way, she said. *It's faint, but the mercenaries came from a different route. Maybe it will hide us from Hillcrest's spies. Yelane is a tricky one. She'll get word out.*

I dug my fingers into the fur along her back to keep myself steady. *Won't we run into the soldier that got away?*

The wolf scent is already fading. They're far ahead of us. Heg lumbered at a slow, plodding pace that lulled my eyes to droop. *Rest, Brin. It's my turn to carry on.*

I sighed in wary agreement. As the sky lightened, I drifted in and out of sleep. My dreams shifted from shadow snakes to sunlit orchards.

You know what would be good with honey? Heg hummed.

I cracked an eye. *Hmm?*

Heg licked her lips. *Roasted quail.*

A hearty laugh rumbled from my chest. *We'll find you some quail, I promise. Just not in Vadril.*

Hegg rumbled in agreement. I pressed my cheek to her fur to hear her heartbeat, and the steady pulse pulled a small smile to my face.

For the first time in my life, I was excited for what was to come.

Want to find out where those peaches come from?

Read *Drizzle*, an exclusive short story!

Acknowledgements

There are many people in my life supportive of my author journey, but for this book specifically, I'd like to take time to acknowledge the long nights, emotional rollercoaster, and overall journey this book took me on. The story of someone expected to put others first and choosing herself was very personal to me, and I think caring so much put a lot of pressure to tell it well.

What I had in my head and what was on paper took several rounds of revisions to refine. A big thank you to my beta readers for their feedback, my family and friends cheering me on from the sidelines, and my editor Clara Abigail for helping me give it a final polish.

I'm very proud of Burn the Bridge, and I hope you enjoyed it as well.

About the Author

Arquie spent her younger years staying up way too late reading books. Let's be honest, that hasn't changed much. She enjoys fantasy novels packed full of adventure and mayhem.

Arquie takes inspiration from her childhood growing up in eastern Montana, too many nature documentaries to count, and discovering niche interests. She looks up to creatives like Christopher Paolini, Kathryn Lasky, James Cameron, and Tatiana Maslany.

Now, she's bringing her own stories to life. You can find her curled up with a good book, hyper fixating on a new hobby, or writing her next adventure.

www.ingramcontent.com/pod-product-compliance
Lightning Source LLC
Chambersburg PA
CBHW030945310726
48969CB00008B/2384